CW01430612

ISBN: 1484896467
ISBN-13: 978-1484896464

Cover Design: Ravven

Edited by: Jacob Neff of Complete Pixels

Contact the Author

The Author would love to hear from her readers and fans. Connect with her on Facebook and she will get back to you: https://www.facebook.com/pages/Jill-Cooper/319251368110396

Or

jill@nosquaresoftware.com with the word 'Reader' in the subject line

Other Books by Jill Cooper

<u>YA Series Dream Slayer</u>
The Dream Slayer: Book 1
Demon Royale: Book2
The Uninvited: A Dream Slayer Novella
Awakening Apocalypse: Book 3 (coming 2013)
Frozen Reverie: Book 4 (coming 2014)

<u>The YA Rewind Series</u>
15 Minutes

<u>Adult Dystopian Series</u>
Glistening Haven
Glistening Rebellion (coming 2013)
Glistening Warfare (coming late 2013)

Plugged (coming 2014)

<u>Romance</u>

Breaching Darkness (2014)
Stolen Kiss (2015)

Acknowledgements

Thank you to Michael Cooper for waking me up at 2AM to ask me what happens next in this novel. It helps to know someone is emotionally vested in what you are writing.

Bonnie Paulson, I don't know where I would be without your constructive feedback and fan girl squealing.

And thanks to Eisley Jacobs for always encouraging me, even when I am clearly crazy.

Chapter One

I have fifteen minutes.

"Lara Crane?"

Standing in the sterile waiting room of the time travel agency known simply as Rewind, I turn towards the voice. Delilah, the redhead technician with a tight ballerina bun, offers me a handshake.

I should be in second period lab class, but instead I cut. I have something more important to do than completing junior year chemistry.

"Nice to see you again." After a glance over my shoulder, I follow her through a tiny hallway and into a secure room. I crinkle paper brochures in one hand and with the other repeatedly tuck my hair behind my ears.

Her lips perch together in a tight smile. "You too, Ms. Crane. One of my favorite return visitors."

I sit down in the overstuffed black recliner, and when she latches the door, the metallic boom makes my heart skip a beat.

This is it. Turning back is not an option.

The stark white walls, sparsely covered with posters, make me feel like a trapped rat. Time travel has rules, the posters warn, and I plan on breaking every one. A daughter will do anything for her mother.

I have one chance at this, and with my heightened blood pressure, it's clear my body knows it. Once you travel back to a specific time, it's catalogued as off limits. Frequent travel to the same moment, in the same space, causes a rut in space, like pacing across a worn floor. If I fail, if I can't do this, my mother will remain dead forever.

The technician is wearing all white, and her shoes squeak against the shiny silver tiles. I've met her before. Her name is Delilah.

She straps the belt around my lap, and my knees bounce up from my bottled-up tension. The clustered nerves in my gut grow larger. I swallow to settle them, but bile rises in my throat.

Delilah sits at her computer a few feet in front of me, probably checking the records for my time travel history. This is my tenth trip, thanks to the frequent visitor discount card Delilah sold me on my second visit. I've been time travelling to plot my route and improve my sprinting time through the city.

She slides over to me on her desk chair. Her eyes search mine, and they glint with distrust. "We checked out the date and location," Delilah says. "It seems like a happy memory. How old were you?"

She's scoping me out. I try hard to keep eye contact. I've worked too hard on this to get found out now. It took every penny I had to pay for this final trip. "I was five. I sang in front of the mayor. My dad was there. It was a big deal to me then."

Delilah slips a standard white hospital-issue heart monitor on my finger and clamps it tightly, catching my skin. With a deft movement of her foot, the chair reclines like the one in the dentist's office, and I'm peering up at the glass ceiling.

She speaks again, seemingly bored now, as she goes through her pockets looking for something until she pulls out a pen.

"You'll have fifteen minutes and will have to watch from the hall."

I nod and try to keep from sweating, but my heart is beating so rapidly it's echoing in my ears.

Her eyes are steady on mine, and her lips pinch together. She recites as if from memory, "No interactions and don't try to meet or touch anyone along the way. You wouldn't be able to anyway."

Or so she thinks. My fingers grip the flyers. Hidden beneath them is a photo of my mom.

"We'll be monitoring you. Any sudden changes in your breathing or heartbeat and we'll yank you out."

Delilah injects my neck with the sleep serum. It pinches like a snapping beetle, and the electrodes surge on my temple. My head tingles. Electricity pulses through my skin, making my foot twitch and my finger clutch involuntarily.

My eyelids are heavy. They close, but the sound of banging forces them open again. I see Rick, my boyfriend, through the window in the door. He bangs the glass with his hand, and I grip the armrest as restraints clamp down on my forearms.

"Arrest him," she hisses into a wall intercom, and armed security guards force Rick's arms behind his back. Delilah turns to me and gives me a smile. It doesn't look friendly.

It's chilling.

"She's ready to go back."

"Lara!" he screams, and the longing, the begging in his voice breaks me. "Don't do this, Lara!"

The chair begins to spin, and the room swirls around me until I'm dizzy with the urge to vomit. The velocity forces my head back against the cushion, and my mouth falls open. I whisper a single word.

"Mom."

****

I open my eyes. I'm standing in the yellow halls of a cheerful school decorated with construction paper artwork. The hall waves in front of my vision as though I'm lost beneath the ocean, and my legs tremble. I slide my feet forward, so I can lean against a locker for support.

I have no memory of what I did before this. I rub my temples. I'm missing something, and my head throbs. I flip through the papers I notice in my hand. It's a pamphlet that says I have fifteen minutes to be in the past.

Time travel?

Flipping through the pages I see short-term memory loss is to be expected but will fade soon. I paid money to go back but why into a school? Something about it is familiar, and I know the hall I'm standing in leads to a music room.

But I don't know how I know any of this. I just do. As if memories were uploaded into my brain.

A photo falls from my papers and lands face up.

Her face. Her eyes. It's like looking in the mirror.

I scoop the picture up and head down the hall. A piano chord strikes. The soft tone echoes toward me, and the digital watch on my wrist beeps. A rush of memories slam into my mind, knocking me off balance. I wobble on my feet as if the collision were physical. I retch, the vomit threatening to spill. Swallowing, it burns like racing lava. I check my watch.

I only have thirteen minutes left.

I don't bother to look through the doors to find five-year-old me. Instead, I race down the hall, feet gliding across the linoleum. My hood flaps behind me as my body crashes into the elementary school front doors. Blinding sunlight greets me, and I am flying down the hill. My arms pump, and I suck in deep breaths of air, like I learned in my time as a sprinter at Cambridge High.

Rounding the corner onto Mass Avenue, I see Tower of Records off in the distance.

Beep.

I now have ten minutes to run eight blocks in time to save Mom. If I don't make it, if I fail, I won't get another shot.

My chest aches, and in my mind, I see Mom. I've seen her in pictures, but my memories of her are pretty much gone. I want to remember her tucking me in bed and cooking me dinners. Now I am alone and have microwaved bowls of macaroni and cheese. Maybe it wasn't Dad's fault. Maybe he did his best, but I want more.

I want a mom.

My legs burn, and my lungs beg me to stop, but I keep going. I push harder and edge my body on until I'm desperate to collapse. A woman steps out from a store. I take a hard right to avoid her, clipping my arm on a brick wall. I groan and pause to bend over with my hands braced on my legs. I take a gulping breath of pain that my lungs reject. The woman comes up behind me and puts her hand on my shoulder.

Shrugging her off, I sprint away.

Eight minutes.

I round the corner toward Tower Records with anxiety tight in my chest.

This is where it happens. This is where Mom's body will be found.

My run slows to a trot as I stop beside the giant music store. I peer up at the towering skyscraper as I round the back, down an alley. Quiet shadows loom around the dumpster. A breeze sweeps by and blows a trash bag open. I catch the stench of decomposing meat, churning my stomach. My head pounds. I groan and grab my temples. Behind me I hear a woman's voice.

"Are you okay?"

Her voice rings a bell only in my deepest dreams. My movements slow as I turn and stare into my mother's face. Her eyes are brown like mine, and her face is framed with curls. The stillness of the sight shocks me. I knew I would see her if I was successful, but I wasn't ready for how my heart would ache or how badly I'd want to hug her.

She has a book in one hand and a cell phone in another. The phone is blinking, suggesting she's been on a call and maybe whoever is on the other end might still be listening. But Mom doesn't seem to care; her eyes are fixed on me.

"I'm fine." Despite my dry mouth, my voice sounds normal, but I am anything but. "Only a headache."

Mom smiles, and her warmth spreads to me. "Well, it's no wonder, back here. Come out on the street where the air is fresh. We'll get you a bottle of water."

I follow her on autopilot and watch her retrieve a bottle of water from her brown leather messenger bag. Around us, pedestrians walk by. Any one of them could be her killer, but maybe being here I've saved her. Maybe I stopped her from going too far into the alley.

I sip the water offered to me, and as she takes it back, Mom asks, "What did you say your name was?"

"Lara," I answer before I can stop. I squeeze my eyes shut. My heart skips a beat with regret.

"That's funny," she laughs. "That's my daughter's name." Her eyes aren't suspicious. Her face is only kind.

My wrist watch beeps. I'm down to two minutes.

Mom turns towards the music store, and I follow. I see a man in the alley out of the corner of my eye.

"Mom!"

Mouth agape, her head whips toward me. "What did you call me?"

There's no time to answer.

A gun goes off.

I throttle her back, and she crumbles to the pavement. I take her place and feel a pinch in my side. My hand covers it instantly, and my legs wobble like jelly. I crash to the pavement, and my knees crunch under the impact. I grimace with my hand over the wound.

For a moment, my eyes lock with the shooter. He has dark hair and brown eyes. His brow furrows, and his lip snarls. Whoever he is, in that brief moment I tremble in fear. Then he takes off running. Around me people scream and run for cover. The ones that don't are by my side. Someone calls for help.

My breath echoes in my ear. Mom is there, taking me by the shoulder. Her lips are moving, but I hear nothing. There are tears in her eyes and mine, too. I fall forward, my head cushioned by her lap. Unable to blink, I can only stare ahead at a red fire hydrant on the sidewalk. Everything grows dim, and my breath rumbles.

I swear I see a shadow leaping over my body, but when I turn my head, no one is there. I don't understand. There was no mugging, so why was I shot? Mom was supposed to be mugged.

Beep.

Time's up. Everything goes dark as when a curtain closes on a stage, but I don't think it's from time travel.

I think I'm dead.

Chapter Two

Darkness surrounds me.

My breaths are labored, and the heat in my side radiates up to my head. I try to open my eyes, but they're instantly pierced by a blinding light. Even if I'm not dead, the intense pain makes me kind of wish I were. Overhead, a bell rings, and the shuffling of feet follows.

Shielding my eyes with my hands, I take a deep breath. I need to remember everything I've done and seen, but my memories are behind a blinding haze. The throbbing will not abide, and something inside me is desperate to come out. I hope it's not vomit. I really hate to vomit.

My eyes flutter open, expecting to see hell, but instead I see a high school classroom. I'm seated at a desk, and the clock overhead reads 2:30. I glance down at my lap. The clothes I'm wearing are someone else's, and her taste is feminine like cotton candy. The hem of the skirt is short, and the shirt is a vibrant pink. I haven't owned anything pink since Mom died and Dad started buying all my things.

How can I be at school when I was just shot outdoors? I should be dying. My hand flutters to my side, but I can't find an injury. Except for the freight train inside my head, I seem to be okay. I sigh with thankfulness. Now I need to go home and see Mom.

"You fall asleep again, Lara?"

Jolted, I turn in my seat. The caring eyes staring at me aren't my boyfriend's but those of Donovan James, one of the richest kids in school. Smart, handsome, and everything handed to him on a silver platter, his life is the complete opposite of mine. He's either ignored me or teased me our entire academic career.

So why is he talking to me now?

His blond hair is perfectly coiffed into place, his blue eyes glow with a spark, and a playful dimple grin greets me.

I shrug. "Maybe a cat nap,"

His smile is weird, as if we're friends. "All those late nights are catching up to you."

The pain in my head makes me squint. "I have a headache. Probably nothing."

"Well, come on. I have some Tylenol in my car." He stands, so I do too, but my stomach churns and legs wobble, so he reaches out to steady me. "Easy there, rock star."

How does he know my old nickname? No one calls me that anymore, not since I was ten. I twist my arm from his tight grip. "I'm fine. You can let go of me."

A crack appears in Donovan's smile. "Must be some headache."

Ending the pain is the only thing that matters to me, so I go. I'll take pain free even if it means spending time with someone I have no desire to be friends with.

We navigate through the crowds in the hall—a mingling of teachers and students. My headache amplifies every sound, every moment, and I'm not too happy with how closely Donovan is following me.

When I think we're free from the high school, my friend Kristine steps in front of us. She has a razor bob, and she's smiling while bouncing on her toes. I fight the urge to tell her to move. I want the medicine, and right now she's only a road block.

"Hey guys." She's so cheerful I want to kick her. "You headed over to Harry's Pizza?"

"We sure--" Donovan starts.

"No," I say curtly, causing both to stare at me with their eyebrows pressed together. "I have a bad headache. I need to go home."

"Home?" Donovan asks in a haunted tone.

"Yeah, home. So I can rest. I need this pain to stop. Sorry, Kristine. Another time."

She nods as if it's no big deal, but there's a disappointed glint in her eyes.

Pushing past her, my vision blurs, and by the time I'm sitting in Donovan's convertible I can barely see anything. There is only the smell of pine, from an air freshener I assume. I feel him put two pills in my hand, and I swallow them dry before he can hand me a bottle of water. I take a big gulp before handing it back.

He plays tennis and always keeps a stash of water bottles in the back. I shouldn't know that, because we've never had a conversation about tennis or anything else. My palms sweat and I rub them on my skirt, what I can find of it anyway. I feel naked, desperate to go home and find some jeans, sweats, anything.

When he puts his hand on top of mine, my body jumps with electricity. I try to pull away, but he steadies me. "Just relax."

Donovan's hand rubs my neck, giving me chills. The good kind or bad, I'm not really sure, but someone other than Rick has no right to touch me. He pulls my hair away, and his lips kiss the nape of my neck. I swat him away and shift in my seat to get away from him.

"What do you think you're doing?" I practically hiss at him.

His eyes shine with mischief. "Helping my girlfriend feel better. At least that's what I thought I was doing."

My insides plummet. I would never date Donovan. What about Rick? My fingernails dig into my thighs. "This headache is bad. I think I better head home." My hand finds the door handle, but Donovan clutches my arm. It's not enough to hurt but enough to make me want to get away, no matter the cost.

"I'll drive you. I'm going that way anyway."

I try not to snarl.

He lives with all the other rich kids on the opposite side of town as I do. He takes me here, not my house. He pulls down a street where all the houses are the same, including the pink rose bushes in front of the entryways. The properties are crammed in with no yards, but at least there are no double-locked doors or screaming coming from apartment B3.

The house he parks beside towers over me. "This *is* my house." Astonishment rolls off my tongue.

Donovan rubs my arm. "Has been as long as I've known you. Feeling better?"

"I am. Thank you for the—"

His lips meet mine. My body goes rigid with surprise. I can't believe this. I'm taken, dating Rick. I feel so guilty to even be with this rich kid instead of the poor one that stole my heart.

I push Donovan away and duck my head down, so he won't see how upset I am.

He sighs. "Lar, I know lately things have been tough, but they'll get better soon."

I can't ask what he's talking about. He has to think I'm the Lara he knows or else I'm in a lot of trouble. "I hope so." I fold the hem of my skirt over and study the stitches. I hope he doesn't see I have no idea what he's talking about.

"Be careful. And I'll call you tonight."

Careful? What could that mean?

"If you change your mind about hanging out, call me and I'll pick you up," he says.

I shrug. "I have chores."

He snickers. "Since when do your parents give you chores to do?"

"Huh...well...see you," I mumble and step out of the vehicle, then hurry up the steps to the front door. A simple wreath of dried flowers and lavender hangs in the center of the purple door. I touch it, remembering what Dad had said years ago about Mom being a hobbyist when they were young. "Mom?"

I'm so desperate to see her, I can taste it. I find keys in my purse and am astonished to find one that works.

A vanilla aroma greets me in the foyer. The house is like a museum and not simply from no one being home, but because everything is so refined. I've never been surrounded by expensive antiques before. The gorgeous furniture has no rips or stains. The living room is decorated with delicate creams and yellow sofas. On the coffee table are fresh flowers and on the wall a mantle of mementos. Everything seems so new, so beautiful but also homey. Someone must have gone through a lot of trouble to make it this way.

In the center of the coffee table is an ornate silver frame. My heart contracts when I see it. The picture is of me and Mom from a few years earlier. We are smiling with our matching eyes and hair, our heads tilted together. Laughter lines our faces. My fingers shake as I touch the frame. It's real. I can feel it.

I need to see her. Now.

An idea strikes me, and I open my purse to pull out my cellphone. A rhinestone case? I balk, but at least I have Mom back. I guess I can put up with being a little girly, but surely no one will suspect if I get rid of some of it.

Scrolling through my contacts, most of the names are familiar. When I come to hers, I freeze. My hands are shaking so bad I can barely slide my finger against the screen.

It rings.

I wait what seems like forever.

"You've reached Miranda. I can't come to the phone right now, but please leave me a message." My heart soars at the sound of her sweet voice.

Beep.

I need to say something. I take a shaky breath.

"Hi, Mom." My voice cracks. "It's me, Lara. Of course you probably know that already." I laugh and wipe my hands on my skirt. "I need to talk to you, so can you please call me back? Please, it's real important."

I'm halfway up the stairs when the front door opens. I turn, anxiously expecting Mom, but two little kids walk in instead. They're wearing matching outfits with deep navy blazers that appear to be a private school uniform. One is a girl and the other a boy, both with hair like sand and eyes reflecting my own cool blue. Warm, familial smiles fill their faces when they see me.

"Can we watch TV before Mom gets home?" The little girl asks me.

Mom? My mouth falls open, speechless. My head throbs, and I squeeze my eyes shut. In my mind I see myself chasing these two through the park, pushing them on the swings, but how is that possible? I only just met them.

Mike punches Molly's arm. Somehow I know their names, as if the memory of them was beamed into my head. "Lara's never going to let us. She always makes us do our homework first."

"Right," I answer with a sigh of relief. "Go do your homework." I ruffle their hair because it feels like the right thing to do.

Still perched on the stairs, I watch them talk as they sit on the floor beside the coffee table and empty their backpacks of books and papers. Their chatter is light and so normal. I grip the railing tightly. All I wanted was Mom back, but so much has changed. I have a family now because I changed one little thing. Okay, maybe it wasn't so little.

I close my eyes and see Rick's face. He's warning me not to risk us, our future. And now I think I have.

Rick.

But I have Mom back.

Chewing on the inside of my lip, I find my room upstairs. I fear it might be a cotton candy palace of princess pink, but the walls are soft white, and the only pink is the comforter on the bed. The room is bigger than the entire apartment I used to live in with Dad. It even has a balcony overlooking our small backyard.

Rooting around inside my closet, I find a pair of jeans and a t-shirt. The shirt is bedazzled with feminine swirls and lace, but it's better than nothing. The label says *Gucci*, and the hoodie I grab is *Juicy Couture*. Everything I own is fancy. Can't I have my stinking Wal-Mart crap back?

I slip them on and my reflection in the full length mirror catches my eye. I look the same, but my hair... My curls are gone; my hair is straight. Why would I straighten my hair? On the dresser there's a flat iron and enough hair products to open my own salon. It makes no sense. I love having the same curls as Mom. Why go through so much trouble to straighten my hair?

Downstairs, the front door slams and I jump.

"Daddy's home!" Molly's voice rings out.

Dad. In my mind, I instantly see my good-natured father, with his brown hair and joyful smile. I wish I could tell him what I've done, but I can't.

I race out of my room and trot down the stairs. I can't wait to see him again and give him a hug. When I reach the bottom of the stairs, he is hugging my siblings. I freeze.

The blond man turns to me.

A stranger.

I turn to ice. "Princess, you have a good day?"

My insides wretch. I want to run. Where the hell is my dad?

Chapter Three

This man, this stranger I had expected to be my father, kisses my forehead and smiles like he knows me, like he's raised me. Vomit rises in my throat.

"I have homework," I say flatly. "When's Mom getting home?"

He checks his gold watch. He's the image of perfection, from his expensive gray suit down to his Italian shoes. I don't know what his name is, but he's gorgeous, and I hate him. It's his fault Dad is gone. I saved Mom for me and Dad, not this guy, whoever the hell he is. He may as well be Satan as far as I'm concerned. I will never accept him.

"Oh, not for a few hours," he answers. Should be before you go to bed. Everything okay?"

"Yeah, I want to see her."

"I'm here if you need to talk."

I nod but can't bring myself to say anything. I hate his sympathetic eyes. I run up to my room, close the door, and lean against it. I close my eyes and take a deep breath, and when I open them again I see a desk with a laptop on it. Finally, something I recognize. I can search for my dad and Rick on the internet, maybe piece together what happened.

The laptop case is pink. Figures. But it's also password protected. What would this Lara's password be? With a deep breath I type *Donovan,* and boom, I'm in.

The background is a picture of me and a group of kids. We're all sitting on a wall at the beach wearing matching tops that seem to be volleyball team outfits. I recognize them, but I don't know them. Except for Donovan. There he is with his arm swung around my shoulder and a dumb grin on his face.

Like he loves me. Like he thinks he owns me.

Groaning, I begin my search. I use WhitePages.com and find Rick easily. He hasn't even moved, but the search for my dad proves futile. I can't find anything on him. I bring up Google and type *John Crane*. There are so many references from across the country I might as well be looking for a Smith or a John Doe. But then I see a news article for Cambridge Massachusetts, and I click on it. The screen flashes and redirects to another page.

Content blocked.

My jaw clenches. They have some sort of Net Nanny crap installed on my laptop. Dad never did this to me. He always trusted me. He knew what kind of girl I was.

Grabbing my sneakers from the bottom of the closet, I head back downstairs. My new dad is sitting on the sofa with the twins and they are going over their homework together. He throws a glance over his shoulder, and his eyebrows furrow. "Going somewhere?"

"Yeah, to find my real dad." My cheeks burn hot and my nose flares.

He stands and the air in the room tenses, contracting around us. The twins stop their homework and look over.

"Where. Is. He?" I cross my arms and stare him down, waiting for an answer.

His eyes are angry but not unkind. "We've been over this, Lara. A million times. I know you wish things were different. Why don't we sit down in the kitchen? I'll make you some tea, and we'll wait for your mother to come home."

He reaches for my elbow. His face is soft and understanding, but I want to wretch all over his fine pressed suit. I yank my arm away and run from the house. His footsteps rush behind me.

"Lara Montgomery, get back here!"

I never even look back.

Chapter Four

It's about dinner time, so the subway is scattered with businessmen and teens heading home. Signs plastered to the interior advertise Rewind.

Want to revisit your son's birth?
Want to store the memory of your wedding?
Join the Memory Bank program at Rewind!

Memory Bank program?

Slouching in my seat, I lurch to the side as the subway stops. The doors glide open, and some people shuffle out while others shuffle in, including an old lady who smiles at me.

I try to return it but can't.

I thought I was ready. I thought I could deal with all the fallout, but this… I wasn't ready for this.

Rick tried to warn me. He tried to tell me.

I remember when we last sat in his room.

****

The comforter is messy and littered with papers. Rick paces back and forth, his hands clasped behind his back. He's wearing a flannel shirt with dancing flames on the shoulder. "What if you get caught?"

"I won't. I know what I need to do. I've been practicing my route."

"That's why you've been out running? Training?"

Our eyes lock, and I see desperation in his.

"When you go back in time, you're a hologram. You know that, so how can you change the past?" Rick says.

I swallow hard. "When I went back on my birthday... I touched stuff while I was there. I helped people. I know I can do this. I know." I shrug. "I think I'm special."

Rick crouches down in front of me, his soft brown hair falling against his brow. His emerald eyes are alive with pain. His hands caress mine. "You know they monitor things from the outside. If they catch any energy spikes or anomalies, they'll end your session, and you'll be arrested. You know that interacting with the past is against the law."

Everyone knows that. Under certain circumstances courts can grant the police the right to go back in time and witness a crime. If that happens, I'm screwed. Lucky for me that process is as exciting as watching grass grow.

"She's my mother," my voice quivers. I close my eyes when he touches my cheek. "Ever since the first time I went back on my birthday--I can't stop thinking about her, Rick." I close my eyes and take a deep breath.

He nuzzles my cheek, and I feel his warming breath against my skin. I'm safe, comfortable.

"I saw how she was with me," I whisper, because if I have to be any louder I won't be able to go on. "I was a baby, and I saw how much she loved me. She sang to me. My dad---we were all so happy." I shake my head. "That's what I want. I need that. He does too."

Rick's eyes soften. "And if you're successful, you know things will change."

"Of course I do. I'll have my mom."

"Not that." He glances away, pain etched on his face. "Your life will change. Our life."

My brow furrows. "What are you trying to say?"

"What if we won't know each other anymore? What if we lose each other?"

The idea quickens my pulse. I brush his soft hair off his brow. "It won't. Nothing could change how I feel about you."

Doubt mars his face. I lean forward and brush my lips against his. Passion comes quick as our lips part, searching each other. I wrap my arms around his neck as he lifts his body onto the bed beside me. He kisses my jaw and rests his head against mine.

"I don't want to lose our future, Lara. Are you willing to risk everything you know for this?"

Rather than answer him, I lay my head on his shoulder. He wraps his arms around me. I'm cocooned and safe.

Despite it all, the answer is yes.

***

I never expected that to change.

It was only the beginning. I had gotten away with changing the past physically, but my heart was paying a hefty price.

The subway lurches to a stop, and I step off onto the platform and head to Rick's apartment. In my old life, his parents would still be at work, and I hope that holds true.

The area he lives in was my home. On the corner, Marv the homeless man passes out fliers. The steps are spray painted, and the streets are dirty and gritty. Everything about my new life feels fake, but this feels real. Like home.

Kids litter the crumbled steps going up to Rick's apartment. I squeeze between them and head up three flights of stairs to apartment 3B. The doorbell is broken, so I rap the door with my knuckles and wait for him to answer. I lick my lips, anticipation building in my belly like a hurricane.

The door opens, but the chain remains latched. Rick's eye peers at me with suspicion. "Yeah?" There is no familiarity in his voice.

My heart drops to my feet, and I find the will to answer. "I was wondering if I could come in and we could talk? It's me. Lara."

"Lara Montgomery?" He's on guard. Defensive.

I want to scream that's not my name, but instead I nod. "Yeah. I have a—I need to talk to you."

"Okay." His voice is uncertain. He closes the door, and the locks spin. "I don't know what you could want to talk to me about."

Letting me in, I notice he's wearing his leather jacket and tight jeans. His hair is in his face as usual, but I can read his curiosity in his posture and walk. He leads me to the living room—cluttered, familiar. Like going home.

His hands are in his pockets, and his eyes are intense, sizing me up. I have to fight the instinct to fall into his arms and kiss him.

"This is going to sound weird, but can you tell me what you know about me?"

Rick's eyes narrow. "Know about you?"

"Where we met? When I moved. What I do at school. Anything you can think of."

"Why?" He scowls, pulling his eyebrows together. He doesn't want to play along.

"I'm having some problems." I decide to be honest. "And I need, need to hear someone say it."

Something in my voice gets through to him. His expression softens, and he takes his hands out of his pockets. "We met at school. Kindergarten. You moved when your mom remarried, all of which you know."

"How old was I?"

Rick turns his head away with a grunt. "This is stupid."

"How old?" I push.

"Seven. Eight. We were kids."

"And?"

"Annnd you promised we'd always be friends, but you got the fancy clothes, the big house. You're in the it clique, so yeah, we're not friends." His eyes darken and his lips curve into a snarl. "You act like you don't even know me."

I sit down on the sofa and cover my mouth. We were priceless. How could that all be gone, like in a blink of an eye?

"You having some sort of mental break or something?"

I shake my head. I can't answer.

He sits beside me and watches.

"Do you know what happened to my real father? John Crane?"

"Don't you?" he counters. "Everyone knows."

Rick is studying me, and I can't give anything away. My eyes dart away from his, but then he touches my shoulder. I melt and my resolve fades.

"I'm having... problems. I feel like I'm living someone else's life. Like these aren't my clothes, those aren't my friends. Like I've made a horrible mistake." I bite my lip and look away.

The coffee table is littered with crap. A wallet. A belt. But no picture frames of us like there was supposed to be. No smiles while stopping for ice cream. No stupid orange teddy bear that I won for him at the fair.

"It's not your fault. Your mom remarried. Look, it's no one's fault you have the good life now. I'd say you're the lucky one." I see bitterness in his eyes and the cavern between us lengthens.

"At least your family is still together." I stare at my hands and see how perfect my fingernails are. I hate my acrylic tips and want to tear them off.

"I thought you liked Mr. Montgomery. You've always called him Dad."

I gawk at him as if he has two heads, and a rush of panic crashes through me. I groan and grab my temples. My brain is on fire. I divert my eyes away, squeeze them shut, and begin to experience a memory. But to me it's brand new.

I'm walking down an aisle in a white dress. My hair is up in a pink ribbon with flower pins. I'm only a kid, and I'm smiling like a goober, tossing pink petals from a small woven basket. Camera flashes blind me on either side. I look ahead to the altar and see Jax Montgomery. He's in a tux with his hands clasped, and he winks at me. There's something in his eye. Adoration. Pride. I'm happy. I can't wait for Mom to say her vows. I can't wait for us to be a family.

The memory fades like fog from a window. My eyes feel as if they're exploding, and I mash my palms against them. When I can open my eyes again I see Rick waiting with a glass of water, which I accept.

He watches me expectantly. I need to tell him something. I sip slowly, to bide my time. Memories of my altered past bombard me, causing intense physical pain as if my body is rejecting them. I'd been told repeatedly what the most important time travel warning is.

Don't change the past.

I knew the risk but took the gamble anyway. Time travel sickness is what they call it. Didn't even sound that bad, only something to warn you off, but I'm beginning to think I bit off more than I could chew.

My hands shake as he takes the glass back. "You're not on drugs, are you? If you are, you can leave right now." His face hardens, but I understand his fear. His brother was arrested for dealing drugs at a school and was still in prison.

Solemn, I stare up into his eyes. "No. Promise. " I try to laugh, but it gets stuck in my throat. "Headaches. I'm okay now."

His eyes narrow on me. "No offense, but you're way different than the last time we talked. You're like, a different person."

Can I trust him? I want to, but this Rick and I haven't been friends in a long time. There's no telling if he will keep my secret or report me. I could spend the rest of my life in jail or worse.

"You ever wonder what life would've been like if I hadn't moved away or become a Montgomery?"

He offers a whimsical smile, progress. "Well sure, when I was little. I wondered when you were going to stop by with your softball glove like you used to." He rubs his knee, and his expression grows serious. He's about to tell me a secret.

I lick my lips in anticipation. I want to touch him, tell him he can trust me, but I can't.

"For years I kept this stupid thing in a shoebox." His tongue clicks against the roof of his mouth, and his cheeks redden.

I know what he's thinking of because I remember it from the past we shared together, when the stupid thing became the first symbol of our love.

"But you moved away," he continues. "I brought it to the wedding. I brought it to the first year of junior high in case I'd see you again, but things were different, and I... never had the guts."

"The lollipop ring," I say softly and watch his face fall and his eyes flicker with anger.

Rick pushes back, increasing the distance between us. "How did you...did my mom tell you about it?"

"No." Anxiety builds in my chest, and I have no choice but to let it out. "You gave it to me. When we were nine."

Rick shakes his head, adamant. "I didn't. Never did. How did you—."

"You did. In a different past. The one I remember. This one, it's all wrong, Rick."

I touch his hand, run my fingers along his as we used to, but he pulls away and is on the other side of the room in a flash. His fingers are tangled in his hair, pushing it away from his eyes that flash unspoken words about me.

I've scared him, and I want to make it right. I stand up, but he holds his hands up to keep me at bay.

"I don't know what you think you're pulling, but I've had enough. You think you can play me?" His face flushes as he glares.

"Rick—"

"You gotta go." He yanks the front door open, and the pictures on the walls rattle.

Twisting on my arches, I stare at him, but he won't look at me. "If you give me five minutes, I can explain. If you can have an open mind—"

"Now!" His eyes are trained at the wall, and his jaw tenses. He needs time, but I am desperate for answers.

Backing through the door, I keep my eyes on his and I see that he feels it. I wait for a sign, but the only one I get is a door slamming in my face. I sigh and exit the apartment building.

It's dusk, and I shiver as a chilled breeze greets me. My stomach is an empty pit. I'll have a lot to answer for at home, especially with it getting so late. But how can it be home without my dad? I should go face the music, but I'm not ready. The longer I wait, the worse it will be, but I can only think about now. I hike over to the subway platform and take the rail over to Mass Ave where the public library is.

It's crawling with college students, so I and my hoodie fit in pretty well. On the second floor, scattered between the rows of books, are computer desks. I slide into one and bring up a search on my father.

Scrolling through the results, some old news articles catch my attention. My breath stops, and my brain grinds to a halt.

Convicted Murderer John Crane denied parole
Ten years ago John Crane was convicted of hiring a hit man to kill his then wife, Miranda. In a botched attempt, an innocent bystander was shot but disappeared before medics could arrive on the scene.

John Crane professed his innocence throughout his trial and incarceration. Email correspondence, fingerprints, bank statements, and voice recordings were enough to convince the jury of his guilt even though the police never apprehended the hired hit man.

Upon his denial for parole, he issued the following statement through his attorney, Fred Grayson, "I am disappointed to be denied parole again, but I will not give up my fight."

Pain pumps through me like blood, surging to every muscle, joint, and fiber holding me together. I doubt I could possibly feel any more pain. It's my fault. I'm responsible. The guilt is mine. My stomach wretches with a convulsion, and before I know it, I'm on my knees, and flashes of white mar my vision. My throbbing brain is again trying to burst from my skull.

From the pain in my head I know I'm about to receive more information than I can handle, and I'm fighting it, which only makes the agony worse. I don't want to know. I don't want to see, but I can only fight for so long.

I feel as if something is jacked into my brain, as if the knowledge is being directly downloaded into me from an offsite source. My body is still in the library, but I don't see the ugly tables or outdated stacks any longer. Instead, I see a blue haze, and when it clears I'm back in the apartment I shared with my parents when I was young.

I'm clinging to Dad's leg. Mom is there too, and she's yanking on my shirt, screaming that we need to go. I'm scared and confused. The police are here to take Dad away, but I don't want him to go. I need him to stay with us.

Dad doesn't say anything. I cling to the fabric of his jeans and bury my head against him. My fingers claw at him, desperate to hold on, and his trembling fingers stroke my hair.

From behind, someone unhooks me and picks me up. I scream and thrash, and over his shoulders my arms outstretch towards Dad.

"Daddy, help me! I don't want to go! Daddy!"

The fear in his frantic eyes scares me. He doesn't make a move for me, because he can't. On either side of him are police, and his face is damp with tears. The officers hold their arms in front of him, so he can't rush after me.

My eyes plead with him. I want nothing more than for him to come and tell me all the whispers I'm hearing at school are a mistake. Daddies don't do the stuff they are talking about. He loves Mom, and he loves me.

"I'll find you, Lara. I promise to God we'll be together again. Damn it, Miranda, you know I didn't do this. You know!"

His words are no comfort. The police hand me over to Mom. I bury my face in her hair and cry as we slip into the backseat of a car, about to be whisked away. What if I never see home again?

The haze clears, and I see the library again as my temples pulse. A few people are gathered around me. I see my purse emptied on the ground, and I scramble for the contents. My phone is vibrating beneath the table with a name on the display.

Mom

I snatch it and realize I need to talk to her in person. A hand clamps my shoulder.

"We called an ambulance," the older man says. He has caring eyes and is wearing an outdated fedora, like Indiana Jones.

"I'm fine. I didn't eat much today." I stand up, clutching my stuff, but my legs wobble.

"You don't seem fine to me, young lady."

"I need to go home." I try to sneak past him, but he shadows my movements.

"Get checked out by a doctor. What could it hurt?"

There's little room for argument, so I wait. Men in white shirts arrive with a stretcher, but I know they won't find anything wrong with me. Nothing that will register on their equipment.

But something is wrong with me. I grip my purse strap and sit down when I'm told. Time travel sickness. The merging of new memories with the old ones. I thought I could avoid it. I thought it wouldn't happen to me, but now it's hitting me and strong.

I need to find my dad. I need to clear his name before all my old memories of growing up with him and being with Rick are wiped out by these new ones. Or worse, before my brain hemorrhages and I die.

Chapter Five

The doctors say I'm okay, only suffering from exhaustion and hunger. But they don't bother to give me a brain scan, and I certainly don't suggest one. Their solution is giving me food and juice. It's bland, but it helps.

Shortly after 8PM, I sit on the edge of the bed and wait for my parents to pick me up. I hope Mom comes alone, so I can talk to her. Footsteps from the hall pull my attention. With anxious butterflies, I glance up and see a disheveled Jax.

His face wears worry. Despite my anger, I remember him from the wedding in my new memory. I have new feelings for him. He raised me, and as much as I hate it, the way I treated him wasn't fair. He's silent as he sits beside me on the cot. His warm hand covers mine, and I study his face as he only inspects the linoleum floor.

I don't want to fight him because I don't want to deal with the consequences of making my life harder than it already is. "Sorry," I whisper and bite my lip.

"Where'd you go?" he asks, his eyes blink quickly and when his eyes lock with mine, they dart away again quickly. It is as if merely being with me is hard. His eyes are filled with hurt I put there, and I'm sorry, for everything.

"Just out. Needed to think."

He shifts, rests his elbows on his legs and leans forward. "Did you use the computer at the library?"

The doctors must have told him everything. "Yeah." I play with the hem of my shirt and I'm awash with guilt.

Jax sighs. "I'm sorry you found out that way. I knew we should've told you about the parole hearing. Your mom…"He trails off, appearing to choose his words carefully. "We didn't want to upset you. Clearly, it worked."

His smile is contagious, and when I return it, he slides closer. He wraps his arm around my shoulder, trying to comfort me. I close my eyes, my insides screaming for him to lay off, but I steady the impulse.

He kisses my forehead. "I'm sorry, princess, real sorry. I know you want to wish it away."

That and a lot more. "Where's Mom?"

"She had a late meeting and was stuck in traffic. She'll meet us at home." He plays with my hair as if he's done so a million times, and I get a flash of his face as he tucks me into bed. My chubby arms hug his neck, and I utter, "I love you, Daddy."

Daddy.

A realization hits me. "Mom works a lot." That I didn't expect. I had thought we'd be together.

"Just for this stretch. In a few weeks we have that vacation to the Bahamas. I know a trip with the parents isn't the trendiest thing in the world…"

I'll have time to spend with Mom, if my brain isn't mush by then. "No, it sounds good. Can't wait."

Jax winks and his face lights up. "I know lately we've had our problems, but I love you, Lar. You have to know that."

"I do. Of course." I wish I knew what he was talking about.

"Let's bring you home. If we hurry you can say goodnight to the twins."

We leave, and his arm guides me toward the family car. Cushioned inside, I watch the scenery fly by and the lights cast their glow across the windows. My phone rings. Donovan. I send it to voice mail.

"You can change the radio station if you want," Jax says.

"No. I'm okay," I say flatly.

He raises his eyebrows.

What else could be different about me? Am I a disrespectful, spoiled kid? Do I take everything for granted now because I have the mom and dad I always wanted, while my real dad rots in prison? I take a deep breath and straighten up as we approach the house. I don't know if he can have visitors, but I have to find out. I need to see him.

The lights are dim and the house quiet when I enter. The twins are probably sleeping by now. I smell potatoes and lemon lingering in the air, and the clink of silverware welcomes me as I step into the kitchen.

There she is.

She's bent over the dishwasher, loading up the evening dishes. Her brown curls are covering her face, and my voice croaks, "Mom?"

She straightens up. Worry and relief fight for a place on her face. My lip trembles, and I rush to her side. Her arms open to accept me, and I crumble against her. I take a deep breath and remember her vanilla scent. She grips me hard, and I do the same, my chest heaving in sobs.

"Oh, baby," she whispers, stroking my hair. "I'm sorry I couldn't call you back today. The meetings and the schedules are crazy right now."

I nod, squeeze my eyes shut, and content myself with resting my face in her hair. It tickles my nose, but I don't care.

She takes me by the shoulders to look at me. Her face is broken with sorrow, and she wipes the tears from my cheeks. "It's harder on you than anyone. If I could make it all go away, I would, Lara."

"I'm glad … that I'm home."

"Me too." Mom smiles and points to the bar stool. "Sit and keep me company for a minute."

She opens the fridge and gets out two bottles of apple juice, handing me one. "When Dad called and told me how you stormed out of the house …" She stops to take a drink. "I was angrier than I've been in a long time, Lara. But when the call came that you were taken to the hospital …" Her face grows pale. "I haven't been that scared since the day in the alley."

I fumble with the lid to my juice. "I didn't mean to pass out or be so…mean."

"I know to have John in jail is hard on you, but Jax loves you too. He's been here for you. For us. And I know you're a teenager, which means your emotions are all over the map. One day you hate us, the next you love us." Mom takes a deep, shaking breath. "I need you to be respectful, okay? It's not easy for him to love you so much and have you slap him in the face."

Have I done this before? "I apologized."

"Good." Seeming relieved, she pulls my hair away from my forehead and kisses me. It's so good to be with her. It's as if I'm basking in the warmth of the sun. "Now head to bed. School day tomorrow."

I want to stay and stare at her, but I agree. From the door I say, "Love you, Mom."

For a moment, her mouth hangs open. "I love you too, peanut."

As I leave the kitchen I see Jax in the living room going over some papers.

"Good night," I tell him.

"Good night, honey." I feel his eyes follow me as I head up the stairs.

Once I'm in my room I change into some pajamas and then analyze my situation. I need to know as much about myself as possible before tomorrow. I notice trophies lining my closet for softball and bowling. Bowling? My nose scrunches. Who does that? My bookcases are lined with romance novels and mysteries. At least that hasn't changed.

Under my bed I find the treasure chest I've been searching for—a photo album. Flipping through the pages I find family photos of me, the twins, Jax. The ones of Mom make me smile. I'm playfully posing in dresses, decked out to the nines as if were some socialite on a mission to rid the world of any color that isn't pastel.

But my face is rosy and alive with smiles. I look happy. Real happy.

A lot of photos are of me with Jax and Mom. I'm placing kisses on his cheeks and helping him blow out the candles on his birthday cake. We are all in fancy dresses, and the backdrop appears to be somewhere tropical or on a boat. I squeeze my eyes shut, and my mind floats back to Dad's, my real dad's, last birthday.

The apartment is so small the kitchen table is butted up against the sofa, and our dog is whining underneath my legs. Dad is tall, strong, and macho, but he's wearing a yellow party hat and a goofy smile. He shakes the wrapped package. "It's not a bomb. Or LEGO."

"Not LEGO." I grin. I'm wearing a comfortable old sweatshirt and no makeup, but I'm smiling. Dad says it's the only makeup I need.

He pulls open the package to reveal some steam engine trains for his model railway. He's been building it for years because he never has any free time or money to spend on it. His eyes go misty in the way only *allergies* can be blamed for. "Lara, this is awesome! Thanks, girl."

I reach across the table, and we hug. In front of us are our finished bowls of macaroni and cheese and a small cake, the flames on the candles dancing in celebration.

"Make a wish," I say and wonder what he's wishing for. I wish for the same thing every year.

He smiles before he blows them out. I clap my hands before he breaks out the forks and plates. Dessert is served.

"What'd you wish for?" I lick the last of the ice cream from my spoon.

"To spend more time with you." He winks and strokes my hand. When he stands up, the chair squeaks across the floor.

Pouting, I watch him pull on his janitor's jacket. Dinner break is over fast this time. "Dad—"

He kisses the top of my head. "It was a great birthday dinner, Lara. We'll talk in the morning before school, okay?"

I force a smile. "Happy birthday."

The sadness in his eyes makes him appear older than he did a few minutes ago. When the door shuts behind him, the apartment echoes with a hollow boom, leaving me cold. Sparky whines and rubs against my leg. I lean down to stroke his fur.

"I'm gonna fix this. I'm going to fix this for all of us."

I take the plates over to the garbage to scrape clean and find a card Dad has thrown out without opening it. Like he does every year. On the envelope is a fancy return address label with a swirling *J* on the corner. I consider opening it to see who it's from. Instead, I respect his privacy and dump our cake on top and move on.

Back in the present, I now wish I had opened the card. I slam the photo album shut, and my cell phone rings. I fish it out of my purse. It's not Donovan, luckily, but Kristine. She was one of my closest friends, and I'm glad some things haven't changed.

"Are you all right?" Her voice is rushed.

"I'm okay," I say with as much enthusiasm as I can muster. "I just got home. I'm tired. News travels fast, I guess."

"It does when it lands you in the hospital, Lara! Musta been traumatic. Are you sure you're all right?"

"Sure as I'm going to be. I'm headed to bed. I'll tell you all about it, tomorrow."

"And any cute doctors you saw, right?" Her voice chirps into a contagious giggle, and I can't help but join her. "Maybe you could call Don to tell him good night? He's really worried. He knows you're ducking his calls."

I cringe. "Sorry. I … don't feel up to it right now. Maybe … you could for me?"

"What?" You would think I had asked her to change a tire. "You *must* want to talk to him."

"I really don't." I squeeze my eyes and hope she won't make a big stink about it.

"Okay, okay. But you better tell me tomorrow what's going on with you two. Especially if it's juicy."

Smirking, I close my phone and glance down at the photo album one last time before sliding it under my bed. It bangs into something.

Curious, I strain my arm under the bed until my fingertips swipe at a hard object. I can barely reach it with my fingertips. If I stretch any further, I fear I will dislocate my arm, but I extend anyway and finally manage to yank it out. It's a small brown chest with a gold belt around the center, but it's not locked. The lid swings back, and I see a small book inside. A diary.

In a flurry, I take it out and flip through the pages. It's my handwriting, all right. I turn to the last used page. Only two days ago.

I bought the dress I want for the prom. Dad took me and we had a great time. He even sprang for lunch. It was nice, just being the two of us again. I love having a sister and brother, but I miss when it was just us. Just the two of us.

Mom's always at work and I'm used to it. I know her work is important or whatever. She can do what she wants. When she's home everyone is clamoring for her attention and I blend in with the friggin wallpaper. Maybe she regrets me. Maybe I'm a reminder of her 'big mistake' with John Crane.

Donovan gave me the prettiest necklace. I didn't realize how he felt about me until I opened that little box. I love him too and I can't wait until prom and we are really alone.

But I can barely concentrate. The men following me are getting closer and the plan is shaping up. I hope they don't suspect what I'm up to. I pray

I scowl at the pages. "What the hell?" I whisper.

Chapter Six

The aroma of bacon and eggs wake me. My usual favorite, but this morning my stomach wants anything but food. My first thought is about my dad. I have traded one parent for another, and the guilt stings like a bee as my alarm clock beeps.

I take a shower, and the water tickles my back. The pressure is much stronger than in my old apartment. Life should be a lot sweeter now. I have all the perks money can buy. But that doesn't absolve me of guilt. It intensifies it.

Mom is alive, and I am thankful one day I will have more memories of her, but Dad is imprisoned. Will I eventually forget the last ten years of memories we've built up together? He cared for me when I was sick, and when we needed medicine he scrimped for change and sometimes went hungry so I could be fed. At some point I might wake up, and that sacrifice will mean nothing to me. Maybe I'll only know him as the one who tried to kill Mom and ruined our happy ever after.

And apparently men are following me. That or I'm insane. I'm sure which option sounds scarier. I'll wait for breakfast to decide.

My hair towel-dried, I wrap myself in a bathrobe soft as a cloud that wicks the moisture from my body. Poking through my closet, I search for something comfortable but come up almost empty. All the clothes are designer labels, and every purse is Coach. I feels more like a Barbie than a person.

I grab a pair of jeans to put on, wishing I could wear the work boots I find in the back of the closet, but that'll alert suspicion, so I slip on glistening pink ballet slippers. A navy blue clinging top completes my ensemble. Lara would wear makeup, but I can only bring myself to apply lip gloss. I slip a headband lying on the dresser over my curly locks and head down the stairs.

Heated conversation between Jax and Mom is coming from the kitchen. Is it about me? I approach the door.

"It's research," Mom says, her voice strained.

"Dangerous research. You promised me you weren't going into memory merging. What if something goes wrong?"

Mom sighs. "We aren't even into the human study. Only seeing if we can do it with the mice."

"If? If? Maybe you should ask yourself if you *should*. That sort of power no human should have and especially not a corporation."

"If it can be harnessed and used to help treat victims—"

Jax's voice seethes with anger. "I don't care what the lofty goals are, Miranda. You need to stop and stop now. Don't you know what's at stake?"

"You have never been through a major trauma. Can you imagine if we could pluck the memory of it from my brain? Lara's?"

Jax sighs "Like I didn't go through it too, right? I didn't help Lara with nightmares?"

"Enough!" Mom says, slamming something on the counter. "You're no longer my boss at work and not here either, so please stop."

Pushing open the swinging door, I see the twins are eating cereal and reading comic books at the table. They talk in strained voices, pretending their parents aren't fighting behind them. Mom and Jax are both at the counter, one putting away dishes and the other pouring coffee, all the while trying hard not to look at each other. They continue glaring at each other out of the corners of their eyes, pretending everything is okay, and I go along with it. I don't want to be in the middle of their argument, whatever it's about.

"Hey squirts," I say to the twins as I reach past Molly to grab an apple from the bowl in the center of the table.

"Hi, Lara!" they echo, but its Molly who twists her head to give me a small, forced smile. "We missed you last night at dinner."

I shift uncomfortably. "Sorry. I had…an errand. I'm here now."

Bustling around, getting ready for the day is Mom, wearing a suit similar to the one from last night.

I'm reminded of the words from my diary—how bitter and neglected I feel. Did I save her so she could go to work? Earn money? No, I saved her for me. Yes, that's selfish. But I. Don't. Care.

Jax pours a cup of coffee, and they both turn to me at the same time. Shock is on his face, and cream sloshes out of his steaming mug.

"What?" My eyes dart to each of their faces. "Is there something between my teeth?" I scratch at my front chompers, hunting for a piece of spinach or something.

Mom walks over. Can she tell something's different about me? Part of me hopes she can. "Your hair. It's been so long since you've worn it like this." She strokes one of my ringlets while I struggle for an answer that won't contradict my previous choices.

"Decided to try something different. Getting tired of all that effort to get rid of my curls. I thought it looked nice."

She smiles and kisses my cheek. "It looks beautiful. I'll be home late tonight. Don't wait up."

I try to cover my disappointment, but her eyes flicker.

"Aww, hon." She reaches out and touches me. "I promise soon we'll do a girls' night. Just us." She fluffs my hair as if this should make me feel better, but it doesn't.

What kind of job could be so important? I never asked Dad what she does, and now I wish I had. My eyes divert to the twins eating their breakfast, and I listen to them talking about school. They're young and impressionable. I bet if I can get them alone, they'll spill their guts.

"Remember what I said, Molly. Stay out of my office. There's things in there you shouldn't see."

Molly nods.

I wonder where her office is. Probably upstairs somewhere.

Mom kisses the tops of their heads, grabs her briefcase from the counter, and leaves only her lingering perfume behind.

Jax drinks his coffee, but his eyes study me rather than the newspaper laid out in front of him. "You better grab your orange from the fridge. Don will be here any minute."

Donovan. My stomach rolls with dread. I forgot all about him. What was I going to do? Break up with him? Right before prom?

I see a plate of nuts on the table and reach for them, but Jax grabs my wrist. "Those are honey roasted. There are some plain ones on the counter."

Thankful, I nod. Last time I had something with honey I ended up in the hospital.

"C'mon, kids." Jax picks up the twins' backpacks. "Don't want to be late for school. See you tonight, Lar."

"Bye, Lara!" they chorus and give me hugs.

I give them a playful smile. "Today we'll have a special snack and maybe even play a game."

Their faces light up.

I plan to pump them for information before anyone else gets home. I pour myself a cup of black coffee and turn on the television while I drink it. The last thing I want after my previous night is to be alone with my thoughts.

On this news is a reporter outside of what looks like the Cambridge branch of Rewind. Do they know something is wrong? The words scroll across the bottom, "Breakthrough at US run Rewind." Curious, I turn the volume up.

"For a while, Rewind has been working on a new service, Jim, as you know—the ability to store important memories. Births, weddings, your graduation, anything you want, for a fee. Then you can revisit it virtually, rather than going back in time. It's cheaper and considered safer because everyone knows there's always a risk of time travel sickness."

"Dangerous stuff. Thank you, Sue. Doesn't this take away from their model of traveling in time? What if these memories were lost ... or stolen?"

"They have their critics, sure, but listen. Time travel is expensive and scary! Plus it's highly regulated and each client must go through an extensive vetting progress that checks brain function to make sure they can handle reliving time. Now there's a cheaper—and faster—option."

"So far we have only basic information about how they retrieve and store these memories. They would be held here in this highly secure, state-of-the-art facility, which I doubt they'll let us tour any time soon." Sue smiles large and plastic like. "Back to you, Jim."

I flick the TV off and drain my coffee. When I've placed the mug in the sink, a horn honks outside. Grabbing my books, in a rush I'm out the door. Donovan is in his convertible with his wrist balanced on the steering wheel. My stomach churns as I slide beside him.

"Hi." I can't believe how shy I sound. What the hell is wrong with me?

Donovan gives me a small smile, brushing my hair off my forehead. "You look real pretty."

A nervous laugh bubbles up. "Thanks."

He leans in to kiss me, but I can't push him away. His eyes close, and mine follow suit. His lips graze mine, making my heart skip a beat. Our kiss deepens, and I slip away, being pulled further into the moment. My body responds as if it knows him, wants him, but my mind shouldn't.

I try to think of Rick. I try to remember what we were, but all I can remember is yesterday and how he looks at me now. I'm no one to him. I'm less than that.

My arms sling over Donovan's neck, and I relax, leaning back in my seat. His arms hold me, caress me, and part of me feels safe with him.

My eyes fly open. What am I doing? What am I beginning to feel? My stomach clenches. I feel as if I'm cheating on Rick, but he's not my boyfriend anymore. Still, I can't settle how angry I am with myself as Donovan's lips move down my neck and across my chest.

Rick was my forever. Now what was I doing? Kissing Donovan because it was expected of me? So what if he's hot? That never mattered to me before. I need Rick, but how can I convince him he loves me if he doesn't? If he won't even take me seriously. I take a deep breath and keep myself from pushing Donovan off of me.

"Missed you last night." He purrs against my cheek, but I resist the urge to run my fingers through his thick, blond hair.

"I had a thing. Sorry." I cross my arms and push a stray hair from my face.

"Your dad told me. Sounds rough, rock star. I'm sorry." He sounds sincere as he starts the car.

So he talks to Jax on the phone about me? It's enough to make my blood boil. Maybe it was an arranged marriage type of thing. Did our parents know each other? But the words of love I found in my diary seemed real enough. Speechless, I watch him out of the corner of my eye.

He's quiet as we drive to school, but his free hand creeps up my skirt. I resist the urge to push it away. Not because I don't like what he's doing, but because I do. Chills run all over my body. I wish he would stop. I don't want Donovan, and I don't *want* to want him. I remind myself I'm not in love with him.

But what if I am? What if I'm beginning to remember that I'm in love with Donovan and not Rick? There's no right answer.

We drive into the parking lot. Kids are everywhere, so we have to drive to the back of the lot to find an empty space.

He turns the engine off and lifts his sunglasses to study me with his sparkling blue eyes. "I'll walk you to class if you want."

I purse my lips. "Sure."

His eyebrows furrow. "Some days I can't read you. You're chilly, but a few minutes ago you were all into it. And last night you didn't return my calls. What's going on?"

I swallow back some spit. "Just a rough night and morning. I was in the hospital late. Can't you cut me a little slack?"

His face shows the hurt of my words, and I wish I weren't so hard on him. His fingers pull at my curls. As he releases them, he watches them spring back into a coil.

"I wanted to make sure you were okay. When I heard you were at the hospital, it scared me. I'm glad you're all right." He edges closer to me, concern in his face.

His words soften me, but I still don't want to kiss him. However, when he leans in, his lips are soft, totally into it, and he massages my arm with his eyes squeezed shut. The passion should be forced; I shouldn't feel a thing, but I melt in his arms again. I try to remember Rick and how much we mean to each other, but as Donovan's hand creeps under my shirt, all I can do is quiver against him.

"We should get to class," I whisper against his ear to break the trance he has over me. I suddenly realize one of my hands is under his shirt, caressing his chest. He has muscles under there I didn't realize existed.

He's smiling, and his eyes regard me softly. "I'm glad you're all right." He gets out and opens the door for me. When he offers me his elbow, I sling my arm through his.

"Do you remember our first date?" I try to play coy, playing with a ringlet of my hair.

He smiles. "If you can call it a date, sure. I mean we were ten, and our parents took us to McDonalds, but we sat at our own table while they had coffee."

I try to hide my discomfort; that was exactly what Rick and I had done. My life seems to have completely erased him and inserted Donovan in his place.

"We cooled for a few years. Junior high was our awkward phase, but when I saw you again in high school … " He leans forward with an I-love-you sparkle in his eyes, and I ache for what I had with Rick. "I knew I had to have you." Donovan closes his eyes and kisses me.

I smile at him. "So we've been together three years. Time sure does go by fast."

"It sure does, and our best years are in front of us." Donovan kisses my hand as if I'm a princess. "You'll see."

"I know," I say, but the optimism doesn't reach my voice. Part of me feels … hopeful. We're silent the rest of the walk to the school. Once inside, he carries my books to my locker through the dimly lit halls.

We are both laughing when I see Rick walk by with a group of friends. I used to be among them, but now I'm a poseur dressed in designer clothes. I am with Donovan, the rich snobby type Rick and I made fun of. I'm so mad at myself as my eyes lock with Rick's, I can barely breathe. Yesterday, I was in love with him, and today I'm making out with Donovan. And it's not the worst thing ever.

What's wrong with me?

Donovan doesn't see my anger as he puts my books away. "How about if I take you out for lunch? We could—" He stops as he sees my jaw tightly pressed together. "What's wrong?"

"Nothing," I snap, yanking my books out of his hands. " I'm going to be late for class." I sling my purse over my shoulder and hurry down the hall.

"Lara, wait!" Donovan screams. When I turn back, he is pointing the opposite way. "Class is that way."

"Of course it is." I snort and storm off.

As I hurry down the hall, something slips out of my notebook. I stop to pick it back up and see it's a birthday card. I flip it open.

Happy Birthday, Lara. I know you're all grown up now, but to me you'll always be my <u>little girl.</u>

I don't even remember where I'm standing until someone touches my shoulder. I turn and see Kristine with her short blonde hair and trendy sunglasses tucked on top of her head.

"We're late for English again. How about we go sneak and have a smoke?"

Smoking? Is there no end to my decadence? "How about we go to English class?"

She snorts with a roll of her eyes. "Fine." Pouting, she trudges along beside me with her arms hanging by her sides like rags. She clearly hates English as much as I hate smoking.

She goes in first and leads me to the back, where we sit together. Mr. Morgan takes attendance while I busy myself with my papers, pretending to be interested. But when he begins his lecture, I take the card out from my book again and inspect every word. The paper stock looks perfect, no finger smudges or crinkles.

Does that mean I hardly looked at it? Why keep it in my locker then? Maybe I didn't believe Dad is guilty, or even if I did, maybe I missed him.

Like I miss Mom.

I leave as soon as the bell rings and head straight for the office to request another copy of my schedule. Once it's printed off, I exit back into the hallway and bump into Rick so hard I send both our books flying in all directions.

"Sorry," I whisper, cringing.

We both bend down, so we can separate our books. He quietly hands me my notebook, barely able to look at me. My heart pounds as his black hair falls over his eyes. In his presence I am myself again. For a brief moment everything makes sense. I am drawn to him and want only to kiss him. I try to forget everything I did with Donovan this morning.

"Thanks." I strain to keep my voice normal despite everything being far from it.

"Sure." Rick touches the overturned card on the floor, but I snatch it up before he has a chance to see who it's from. "Boyfriend, right?"

I'm angry that he thinks he has me pegged without ever having the chance to know the real me. "Right, because that's the only person I could ever care about." I tuck the card inside my books and stand up.

"Okay, okay. Relax," he says, holding his hands up in surrender. He comes over to me and looks at the papers in my hands. "Why do you need a class schedule? School's almost out." His eyes darken, and before I can think of an answer, he interrupts my thoughts. "You really don't remember, do you?"

Suddenly, the idea of him believing me, telling him everything, terrifies me. Someone else will know how epically I have screwed up the universe. I'll be held accountable. I'll be forced to fix it, or I'll get into the type of trouble you can't talk yourself out of.

Rick's eyes grow cool. "Last night you wanted to tell me some big secret, and now you want to blow me off?" He snorts. "Whatever, Lara. Not sure why I ever bothered with you." He slings his backpack over his arm and continues past me. He allows his shoulder to hit me like I'm nothing but an obstacle on his way.

His words cut me. "Wait!" I chase after him. A few students are here and there, but they are easy to duck, and I catch up to him around the vending machines.

He stops, eyebrows arched in wide-eyed amazement. "I never took you for a sprinter."

I cross my arms and wear my best defiant expression. "There's a lot about me you don't know."

He nods. "Listen, if you're going to be drama all the time—"

"I'm not drama," I say with a smile. I can't keep the laughter out of my voice.

His eyes sparkle with amusement, acceptance. "You said if I gave you five minutes you could explain all of it to me."

I nod, lick my lips, and dig for the courage to tell him, the sort of courage I only get from peering into his eyes. "You can't tell anyone. It has to be a secret."

"I'm good at keeping secrets, as long as no one offers me a hot dog."

I'm reminded of a memory of his older brother bribing us. We won two hot dogs out of the deal, good ones with mustard and ketchup. It didn't get much better than that. We had to keep quiet, and we did, but we had no idea the secrets were serious. They were about drugs.

"If we go somewhere we can—"

"Not so fast," says Principal Newman, coming from his office around the corner. "Don't you children have class?" He has raised, overgrown eyebrows and black tip glasses that slide down his nose so his wide brown eyes drill through me.

I stutter, searching for an excuse, but Rick holds up his hands in defeat. "Sorry, Mr. Newman. I'll head to class."

He stares us down with his hands clasped behind his back, lips perched together in victory. I glance over my shoulder at him as we walk away and realize Rick is touching my shoulder. I stare up at his face, lips parted, thinking he's going to kiss me.

"Sorry, I can't get another detention or my mom is going to start storing me in the meat locker at the butcher shop she works in. After school, the old footbridge by the Charles River. Maybe we can meet there?"

"Sure, see you there."

Rick gives a sly grin. "Good. And then I'll decide if you're crazy or not."

He starts off down the hall, and I watch after him, wondering if I'm ready, wondering if I can really trust him.

***

Thankfully, I'm able to spend study hall in the library and sign up for some computer time. Once online, I use news media sites to research articles on Dad. I skim old articles about his trial and sentencing, looking for information on where his sentence is being carried out.

My eyes skim over the words as I steel my heart the best I can, but phrases about his love for his daughter grip me. He protested his guilt, begged the courts to realize he was framed. Even to me his words sound like the insane ramblings of a desperate man. I can only conclude that someone did frame him. It's the only notion that makes any sense. But who it was, I don't have a clue. I come to another article.

John Crane Injured in Jailhouse Fight.

It's dated less than three days ago. My mind is frantic as I wait for the page to load. I lick my lips and take a sip of my bottled soda, but its flat and barely sweet.

John Crane, serving twenty-five to life for the attempted murder of his wife, Miranda Crane Montgomery, was shanked during a cafeteria prison riot.

Seated by himself, security officials state that when the fighting started, he tried to break up the commotion. His defense attorney requested that the courts move him to a more secure facility. Court papers are sealed, but insiders report that Mr. Crane suspects someone is trying to kill him to keep the cover on the attempted murder of his wife over ten years ago.

Pending a hearing, John Crane is being held in protective custody at the maximum security prison Cedar Junction.

I sit back and take a steadying breath, close the article, and look up the phone number for Dad's defense attorney, Mr. Franklin. As I type it into my phone, my hands are shaking so badly I'm afraid I'll drop the phone as I put it to my ear.

"I need to talk to Mr. Franklin."

"I'm sorry. He's in a meeting."

The librarian is glowering at me and points to the *No Phones* sign hanging above her desk. I ignore her. "Tell him it's Lara Crane. I want to see my father."

"One moment please."

The bland hold music plays for an eternity while I wait for him to come on the line. "Ms. Montgomery? What can I do for you this time?"

This time? "I want to see my father."

"Well, this is a first." His tone suggests that I am an annoyance, someone he's forced to put up with. "What's with the change of heart?"

"Can I come see him or not?"

"Are your parents aware you're making this call?"

"Nope," I say with as much angst as I can muster. "Is that going to be a problem?"

He sighs and I hear a tapping noise on the other end.

"I know he wants to see me, and he was hurt, so let's get this done and worry about everything else later."

"Is tomorrow morning too soon for you, Ms. Montgomery?"

"Perfect. I'll come to your office." I snap my phone shut, and the librarian slides a detention slip onto my desk.

Chapter Seven

Principal Newman isn't happy with me, but I promise not to use my phone in the library again, to appease him. He mentions my recent troubles, which makes me wonder what I was doing before I jumped timelines.

School is almost out for the day, so I go back to my locker to switch out my textbooks for my notebooks. I'm about to leave when I see Donovan walking toward me. My heart leaps, and my hands are instantly clammy at the sight of him ... but part of me tenses. I smile and wave. I feel bad that I'm planning to meet with Rick, as if I'm somehow cheating on Donovan.

God, what is wrong with me? I'm going mental.

He moves in to kiss me, and I tilt my head back, almost welcoming it. His arm is around my shoulder, pulling me close. I open my eyes and catch our reflection in the window from across the hall. There I am in expensive clothes that aren't mine, kissing a boyfriend I have no right to, and the expression on my face makes me gag.

Bliss. Love.

"Whoa, what's the matter?" Donovan asks.

I push myself away, my hands running my hair back. "I can't do this."

"This? This what, Lara?"

I point between us. "This. Us."

His features widen. "Don't make jokes."

"It's not a joke. I can't ... look at us," I hiss. "Just look!"

He steps forward. "You are not making any sense. What I see are two people in love, having a good time—"

"Two rich, good-looking people, right? You have the fancy car. I have the designer bag, the Gucci bag." I throw it down on the floor in a fit. "None of this is me. None of this is supposed to be mine. Don't you get it?"

Donovan lets out a long breath. "I get it, okay? I do."

"How?" I ask the impossible.

"It's about your dad, right? The life you would'v had if things hadn't gotten so out of control."

"Yes." I can't believe how well he knows me. "I'm not supposed to be in these rich clothes. I'm supposed to be struggling to survive. Meanwhile, all my old friends ..." I bite my lip. "I left them. I betrayed myself."

Donovan shrugs. "Like if they were the ones that traded up, they wouldn't have done the same thing."

My eyes widen, my heart burns with anger, and my lip snarls. "Traded up? That's no way to talk about someone's father."

"Look," he says, anger creeping into his voice, "you were a kid. What were you supposed to do? Say no to the toys and clothes Jax wanted to buy you? Were you supposed to sit in the corner by yourself and not make friends? Stop being so hard on yourself, Lara."

I squeeze my eyes shut and swallow hard. It can't be that easy. Maybe once, but knowing how much love I had with Rick once, I couldn't turn my back on it.

"If I wasn't a Montgomery, if I didn't have the fancy clothes, would you still want me?" My voice strains.

But Donovan never breaks eye contact. "Of course I would."

He says it with such confidence I have no room for doubt, but it's not true. Before I changed the past, he never even looked at me, but he believes it and that's saying something.

Donovan takes me by the arm. "A bunch of us are going out for burgers and fries. You should come with us. Relax. Calm down."

"I made plans to meet someone I knew a long time ago. Catch up. Tomorrow, I'm all yours."

Donovan twitches beside me. "So that's what this is about? Reconnecting with an old friend?"

I shrug. "Maybe."

He takes both of my hands in his and kisses them. "If that's all it is, go and have fun, but don't tell me you're giving up on us. I couldn't stand it."

Glancing away, I sigh. "Don ..." Before now I have never called him that. Parts of me all over are softening to him. Boy, are they ever.

He brushes a strand of hair from my face. His hand is soft as it strokes my cheek. My eyes close briefly. "Tell me you're still my girl, Lara."

I take only a moment to answer, and my heart stills in the moment. "I'm still your girl."

Do I mean the words? I can't be sure.

Donovan kisses me, his arms tightening across my frame. I can barely catch my breath against the whirlwind passion that engulfs us. This time he is the one to pull away, and I tighten my arms around his waist, refusing to let him go.

"I'm sorry," I finally whisper against his cheek. "I was afraid, and I'm sorry."

He smiles. "We're all allowed to get scared some times. Even you, Montgomery." Donovan winks at me.

I start toward the front of the school, ready to meet Rick.

I have no idea what I'm doing.

My heart feels torn in two.

****

I walk to the Charles River and find my way to the footbridge. The river is swarming with sailboats, but the bridge is quiet for a Tuesday afternoon, with only a few joggers using it to cross the busy street. Below it I find Rick leaning against the tan support structure. His head is tilted as he plays with a device in his hand. He seems a million miles away.

His head snaps up when my shoes crunch on some fallen leaves.

"Hey."

He gives me a timid smile and stuffs his hands in his pockets. I haven't seen him act this shy in years. "Was beginning to think you weren't going to make it."

"I was held up, sorry."

He nods. I can see nerves bubbling out of him. Added to my own, this is going to be one game-changer of a conversation. "Sorry about yesterday. It just freaked me out." His hands fan out in a display of surrender.

"It's all right." I smile. "I shouldn't have said anything. I shouldn't have even come to your house."

He shrugs. "Today I was thinking, somehow you knew about the ring even though there was no way you should. And if my mom didn't tell you … how'd you know? So I guess I'm here out of curiosity. I need to know if you're for real." His eyes narrow, glinting at me.

I want to be an open book. We feel like strangers, and I hate it. He's standing so far away, and his posture says all the wrong things. All I want is for him to hold me, kiss me. But then I think of Donovan. Maybe we have a good thing. Maybe I should give it a chance.

Maybe …

"All right," I say, trying not to sound as if we're playing truth or dare, but there's an edge to my voice. "I'm from a different past, and this future is all messed up." I laugh. "Royally messed up."

"How?"

He hasn't told me I'm insane yet, so that's a good start. "Well for one, in this one we're not a couple."

His eyes twinkle with mischief. "Us? A couple?" He thinks I'm joking, but I could never be that cruel.

"I never moved away. We grew up together in the same apartment building. I live with my dad and our dog." I take a deep breath, pain rippling through me. "My mom was killed in that alley all those years ago."

Shock ripples through his face, and his mouth falls open. Even his hands fall from his pockets. "Your dad got away with it?"

My lips twitch to the side, and anger grips my chest. "He's being set up. He's been in prison all this time here, and it's my fault."

"How is it your fault?"

He's trying to read my expression. In my timeline he would know exactly what I'm feeling, but I'm not sure if it works the same here.

"Time travel? You went to the agency?" His voice is tight with disbelief.

"Yes, and you can stop looking at me like that now." I lick my lips. "I know it was dangerous. I know it was—"

"Stupid," Rick finishes for me.

"I wanted my mother." My lips pucker. "But I didn't think I'd lose you, my dad, gain a sister or a brother." I wipe my hair from my eyes.

Rick's eyes narrow. "It's impossible to change time."

"Not for me, it's not," I snap back. "We've already had this conversation. You just don't remember it."

He rubs his lips. "You can't expect me to believe——"

"You, no, but the other Rick …" My voice drops to a whisper. "… would never doubt me."

"This is messed up." Rick huffs, and I see him the way he is with others who don't know him. Tough. Distant. It hurts me to have him act that way with me. "You know this secret side to me that you shouldn't, but I can see it in your eyes."

"See what?"

"Familiarity." Rick spits out the words. "You know me in impossible ways. No one gets close to me. No one. And you're looking at me like I'm some sort of puppy dog."

I laugh and glance away. "Well, you think you're pretty tough, but once someone gets to know you …"

He steps closer. "No one gets to know me. That's the point. That's how I like it."

His face is close to mine, and his stern expression is beginning to crumble in front of me. "Liar. You say that, but you don't mean it. Like when your brother went to jail. You said you didn't care, but people don't cry over stuff they don't care about, Rick."

His lips pinch together. "Never happened."

"Right," I say dryly.

His eyes aren't merely studying me anymore. They are boring holes, as if he's searching for my soul. "Your face, your hair, everything about you is the same," Rick whispered. "But your eyes … something about them isn't right. They're not the Lara who has been avoiding me for years."

My heart pounds, anticipating his touch. If he does touch me, I'm not sure how I will stand it. My eyes close as he brushes my jeans as his hand runs up to my shirt.

"These clothes, they aren't you." Rick shakes his head. "It's like they don't even fit you. They look …"

"Fake?" I whisper. "Everything about me feels fake."

Rick's glares until I can barely see the white of his eyes. "You really did it. I wish I could remember."

"Me too." The words nearly crush me.

We both stare down at my hand resting on his chest.

"If you expect me to start kissing you ..." Rick says. "But part of me wants to, to see."

"See?"

"How it will feel. If we were together before, maybe ..."

"Rick?" I whisper.

"You were the only friend I had. When you left, things were hard. I missed you. Then my brother went to jail, and I was more than alone. I was ... abandoned. I thought when we met up again in junior high you'd say something. You'd be there for me. But instead, you walked right by me, like we didn't mean anything to each other at all."

Rick shakes his head and turns away, staring at the river. I hear the squeal of children running through the grass, and the wafting aroma of hot dogs cooking makes my stomach rumble with hunger. I can't even remember if I ate lunch.

I blink back tears. "I'm sorry I was so cruel."

"I know you're the same person, but you're really not. I was never attracted to her but to you." Rick's hand lifts to stroke my cheek but stops short. "Maybe if you weren't with the prick."

Donovan. I forgot about him. "He's not a ..." I shake my head. "He's not so bad once you get to know him."

"Now what?" Rick asks after an eternity of silence.

"I don't know. Other than find out who is framing my dad and get him out? I don't know. It won't change the time we've lost, but I can't let him stay in there."

"And you're going to do that how?"

I shrug. "Going to go see him. I have to start somewhere. Even though nothing will ever be right here, I have to help him before ..." I hadn't meant to tell him quite this much.

"Before what?"

"My mind melds completely with this timeline." I take a deep breath. "I'm remembering things I shouldn't. Headaches come, like the one you saw me have yesterday. I knew ... it was a danger. I didn't think—"

"But you did it anyway?" His eyes narrow. "Do you ever think about consequences?"

"Sometimes," I offer with a shrug.

He jerks away when I try to touch his arm. "It makes me uncomfortable. You know all these things some other version of me told you, and you're looking at me like you expect something of me. Like what? Should I fall back in love with you? Because you told me that's how things are supposed to be?"

"No." For such a small word, I choke on it big time. "It wouldn't matter. You wouldn't have any of my memories—sitting at the beach, that time you cheered me up by taking me to the zoo and roaring with the lions. It'd be ... meaningless. Without those memories ..." I shrug.

I'm so heartbroken, and the air is so thick, I gag on it. My senses intensify. The grass seems greener, the air is cooler, and my breath more labored. I close my eyes for a moment, and when I open them again Rick is watching me with pools of pity.

It makes me sick and puts a metallic taste in my mouth. "Better go," I whisper. "Not sure why I thought this was a good idea."

"Wait a second, Lara." His tone slows my marching feet, and I pause without turning back. I don't think I could stomach looking into his eyes one more time today.

"If you need help, with your dad. Well, let me know. What I do remember is he was good to me, so let me know."

Taking a deep breath, I nod. I try to say thanks, but nothing comes out. Instead, I start walking. I leave the river, heading toward the closest T stop, but my feet are sore and I'm exhausted. I stand on the corner and wait for a cab.

The hairs on the back of my neck go up, and when I glance back, I see two men. They both are wearing leather coats with sunglasses, and one has a tattoo of a gold dragon going up his neck. Whoever they are, they are bad news, and I can't help but think of my diary entry as I watch them cross the street. If they don't change their trajectory, they will be on me in seconds.

I flag down a cab and give him my address, happy to be safe. The back is air conditioned but smells of mold and old socks. I go through my wallet to find cash, but all I have is my credit card. That might come in handy. I pull it out and something wedged behind the plastic falls out.

A key.

Chapter Eight

I'm the first one home, and I make a mad dash for the kitchen. I pour two glasses of milk and find a big platter to lay out cookies and candies. I don't know what Mike and Molly like, but I'm sure no kid can resist a bribe made of sugar. I place the platter on the table and get out some napkins. Another sweep of the kitchen and I spot the morning newspaper Jax was reading so intently.

I smooth the wrinkles and read the first page headline:

"CONGRESS TO VOTE ON TIME-TRAVEL BILL"

Senator Patricia James has put forth a bill allowing select police officers to travel back in time to verify witness testimony and hunt down dangerous suspects. Currently, the police need to petition the courts for access using a time-consuming process. Critics argue that frequent time travel will scramble the officers' brains and interfere with the due process afforded to individuals charged with crimes. The bill is set to be voted on early next week.

Senator James was one of the founding members of Rewind before being elected to public office four years ago. She has made it her life's mission to thwart dangerous crimes by providing safe time travel for officers of the law.

Senator Patricia James.

James.

Wasn't that Donovan's last name?

I jump when the front door slams. A chorus chimes out from the kids. "We're home!"

Their nearly identical faces smile at me, and I come back with a grin of my own. "Hi, kids!"

I swoop down to give them big bear hugs, and I'm crushed under their embrace. I can't help but feel the warmth and love that bubbles from them to me. Their faces are all chubby cheeks and glowing eyes, and they smile infectiously. Mischief skips across my lips as I give them kisses.

"I have a surprise for you guys. Follow me."

I take each of their hands in mine and lead them into the kitchen. As they see the table, smiles break out.

"Yay!"

They make a break for their chairs. The legs are grating against the floor before I can even sit down. They each put a cookie on their small saucers. Molly slowly and deliberately dunks hers into milk, while Mike shoves the entire thing into his mouth.

I sit with them and take a bite. "How was school?"

Molly goes first. "Good. We read about dogs, and I worked on my subtraction tables."

"Handwriting is lame." Mike shrugs. "We use computers most of the time anyway. Who cares if I can sign my name?"

"Legal documents. It's nice to know."

"I guess." Mike goes back to drinking his milk.

"Want to watch a movie after? What's your favorite?"

"*Tangled!*" Molly says and gives me a smile revealing two front teeth. "No, no, *Brave!*"

"Oh, not again. I'd rather watch *Iron Man*," Mike says.

My eyes narrow, but I keep my tone playful. "Are you allowed to watch *Iron Man*?"

Molly giggles and points at him, and he slouches further down. "No."

"We can find something the three of us like."

Molly giggles again, this time pointing at me.

"What's so funny? Do I have crumbs on my shirt?"

"No, but duh."

I try not to laugh. "Duh?"

Molly nods, but Mike is the one who speaks. "Movies, plates of cookies. You want something."

"Uh-huh!" Molly says, but it doesn't stop her from taking another cookie. "I like it when you want something."

"Okay, okay." I sigh, realizing my approach isn't working. These kids are too smart for their own good. "You're right, but it doesn't mean I don't love you." As I say the words, they ring true. I do love them even if I barely remember them.

"Maybe we can help," Mike says. "Like that time we helped you sneak out to see Donovan after dark."

My lips twist to the side. "Okay, but it stays at the table, or I'll tell Mom about that time you threw your dinner down the garbage disposal." I figure they are young, this must have happened at least once.

From the fear in Molly's face, I have her pegged as the guilty party. Her eyes open wide, and her mouth drops. "Okay, okay! We promise!"

"Good." I smile. "I wanted to talk about Mom for a few minutes."

They exchange nervous glances but stay silent.

"It makes me sad she's gone so long."

Molly nods. "Me too," she whispers.

"But we don't want to make her feel bad," Mike says quickly. "We hate when Mommy's sad."

"Me too," I admit, and my nose scrunches into a ball. "Maybe we should surprise her with a special present. Show her how much we love her."

The kids start bouncing up and down in their seats, and I know I have them. "I could take you shopping tomorrow after school. Maybe swing by your school and we can go together."

Molly giggles. "I love the mall! But Mom says I'm too young to hang out there by myself." She pouts with her bottom lip protruding out.

"Well, she's right about that." I play with a cookie on the platter. "What does she like? What do you guys think would make a great present?"

The kids look at each other as if they are reading each other's minds. "Mom likes cats."

"You like cats," Mike tells Molly. "She's always out late. Maybe we should give her a gift certificate to a restaurant."

"Or a spa," Molly adds.

"No, no." I sigh, agitated, then snap my fingers. "That's a bad idea. I mean a gift from us, from our heart to hers, not a piece of plastic money. That's what you buy a teacher or your boss."

Molly's lips curve down. "I thought it's what you liked." Her voice is hushed and small. I watch her little face scrunch up, about to dissolve in a fit of tears.

"Oh, Molly." Crestfallen, I reach over and hug her, plopping her down on my lap. "I do, normally. I want this gift to be extra special." I stroke her hair back, and her tears taper off. She snuffles back the last of her running nose.

"It's a gift. Isn't that special?" Mike asks.

"Even more special than Christmas," I say, eyebrows dancing with exaggerated excitement.

Molly looks up at me, eyes growing wide. She fidgets until she's off my lap and running from the kitchen. I throw confused eye darts at Mike.

He shrugs. "Girls."

Molly runs back in and hands me a flyer. "I saw Mommy looking at this one morning before work."

I smooth out the paper's wrinkles and see a silver necklace. It has a heart pendant with birthstones attached to the front. "This is great. We'll go tomorrow to the mall and then bring it to Mom's work. You guys know where that is?"

Molly giggles and covers her mouth while Mike rolls his eyes at me. "We all know."

"Sure you do," I tease. "But if you don't tell me, how am I supposed to know if you know?"

Mike narrows his eyes and blurts out, "Rewind. See, I told you I know."

"Mom …" I feel the color drain from my face, and my stomach wretches., "… works for the time travel agency?"

Mike nods. "You really didn't know?" Molly asks. "But we've been there," she rushes on. "We saw Mommy in her white lab coat, and she told us—"

"Not to touch anything," Mike says. "Her experiments and research are important, and she doesn't want anyone to mess them up."

"But she's almost done!" Molly's shoulders scrunch up to her ears with excitement. "Then we can go on a vacation with water slides!"

"Yay!" they both cry out, throwing their arms up in the air while I desperately try not to puke.

Our arrangement is forgotten as they run to the living room. I put the cookies away, trying to piece together what this means before I join them. I find them on the sofa, arguing over who gets control of the remote.

"Remember," I say, wiping my hands on my pants, "it's a surprise. So don't tell Mommy or Daddy."

"*Or* Daddy?" Molly asks, mouth falling open. "But, how will you get us out of school?"

"I have my ways." I wiggle an eyebrow at them and plant a kiss on each of their heads.

Mike looks up at me, his brown eyes like Jax's, staring right through me. "Can we get McDonald's at the mall?"

"Happy meal!" Molly choruses.

I love their little faces more than anything. The love tugs at me, and I wonder how my life was ever complete without these little monkeys. "I'll get you anything you want as long as you don't tell."

They promise, hands over their hearts, and I retreat to my room to do my homework.

And to think.

****

My homework is laid out in front of me. I try to concentrate on it, but I've read the same page four times, and the end of my pencil has snapped off.

Mom worked for Rewind. I scour my brain, trying to find a memory of that, but I can't. I can do little else than fret about what this means. Why is Mom always working late? What project is she close to finishing? And how does this tie into our past? Maybe tomorrow I can get some answers from Dad, but until then my brain is going to whirl with wonderings and horrible *what if* scenarios.

At this point, Rewind is my enemy. If they find out what I did, I'll be arrested. Or worse, they will try to fix the mess I created. But maybe that's what should happen. Maybe, but I'm not ready to let Mom go. We haven't spent any time together yet. My mind floats back to six months ago, the first time I went back in time to see Mom.

****

Dad is buying me the time travel package as a present. I know how much it's costing him, but his face is glowing as we step inside the sterile agency. The walls are pristine white and the furniture is unnatural silver, comfortable but stark to the eye.

I clutch the brochures while I study all the information laid out in them about time travel sickness and what would happen if you try to affect the past, but luckily such a thing isn't possible, or so the brochures tell me.

Dad sits on the sofa beside me and keeps crossing and uncrossing his legs and rubbing his neck. I'm not sure what he's nervous about. I'm the one attempting time travel for the first time, and my stomach is a bubble of nerves.

A lady approaches with severe red hair clipped back in a tight French twist that makes her face look like a stretched marquee. We stand and she shakes Dad's hand. "Delilah, thanks for taking us so quickly," Dad says.

She smiles and squeezes my hand. "Make yourself at home, John. I'll bring her back when I'm done."

I look back over my shoulder and Dad grins, but he seems nervous as he walks over to the magazines.

I didn't notice it then, but now it's obvious to me that Delilah and Dad knew each other prior to that first trip to the agency. They were never introduced. They knew each other. But I was so excited about seeing Mom that I didn't even think about that.

****

I follow Delilah into a private room and try to relax in the overstuffed recliner. She busies herself around the room before slipping a heart rate monitor on my finger. She spins a few dials on a computer and speaks without looking up.

"The past can see you, even talk to you, but you're like a hologram projection into their minds. You aren't able to touch them, take a bus, or even open a door." She gives me a sad, haunting smile. "I know why you want to see her, but you won't be able to touch her."

I nod. "Dad told me."

"Good." Her smile is back, pushing up her cheeks and exposing her dimples. "If you tried, you'd set off alarms, and we would pull you out. I'm not saying we'd arrest a kid, but we can't make exceptions."

"I get it." I bite my lip as my nerves flitter around inside me.

She places electrodes on my forehead. "Close your eyes and take a few deep breaths. You'll be dizzy when you get there. Remember, all you have is fifteen minutes."

Laying my head back, I think of my mother. I can barely remember her face. If it wasn't for pictures, I would have no memory of her at all. Her voice was once sweet, and her laughter pure, but now it's almost as if I'm watching a silent film in my head. All I want is to recapture that, and thanks to Dad, I could.

"Happy birthday," I whisper to myself, and the chair began to spin. When I open my eyes I'll be with my mother again, like magic.

****

I open my eyes and see my homework laid in front of me. My nose feels wet, and a few drops of blood splatter to the pages. I can't remember the last time I had a nose bleed. Rummaging through my desk for a tissue, I notice my hand is laced with traces of blood. I guess I'll have to work faster if I want to free Dad before my brain hemorrhages. I glance at the clock. Where did the last three hours go? I can't remember.

Swallowing my fear back to the furthest corner of my mind, I run to the bathroom and get a washcloth. As I'm running it under the tap, I hear footsteps. I hold the cloth to my nose, and a light knock comes at the door.

"Just a second—"

The door opens anyway. Mom, still dressed for work, enters with an alarmed expression.

"When did this start?" She takes the washcloth from me and orders me to sit down on the toilet.

I do as she asks and tilt my head up, staring into her warm eyes. She keeps my nose clasped tight and pats some cool water on my cheeks. This is what I missed growing up. I love my dad, but he was always making sure I was self-reliant, which means if I was hurt, I patched myself up. He was probably working anyway.

"A few minutes ago, while I was doing my homework."

Mom twists her lip and chews on it while her eyes stare off at the wall. When I straighten my head, she releases my nose. The bleeding has tapered off, but she won't let me go yet. She washes my face clean and then plants several small kisses on my forehead. I put my arms around her waist and bury my head in her stomach. It's the first real moment we've had together. She strokes my hair, seemingly incapable of keeping her lips to herself. Her hugs are urgent, full of worry. "Tomorrow, I'll call your doctor, make sure everything's okay."

"Mom—"

She holds up her hand.

I'm not going to win this battle.

"Get some sleep. We'll talk tomorrow, okay?" One more kiss on my cheek and she's off.

I look back at my reflection in the sterling encased mirror. I'm not ready to give her up. Not ready at all.

Chapter Nine

In the morning, I leave early to avoid questions and end up in an expensive-looking blue sedan. We head toward the prison where Dad has lived for the past ten years. Mr. Franklin seems okay enough, with the face more of a warm grandfather than a ruthless lawyer. I wish Dad had the best council money could buy, but it seems he doesn't. My blood turns to ice as I realize his situation is all my fault.

Mr. Franklin escorts me into a room where I am asked to fill out and sign several forms. After a while, I get a visitor pass and attach it to my sweater. The lawyer and the guards exchange head nods, and Franklin signs his name. He rests his hand gently on my shoulder.

"You sure you're ready for this? If you're having second thoughts …"

I shake my head. "I'm ready." I take a deep breath to steady myself. The door in front of me buzzes, and it's opened by a police officer with a neck thicker than my waist. Apprehensive, I will my legs into the small room. Once I do, the door latches behind me.

There are three chairs to choose from in front of a glass wall separating me from the prisoners. I take the third seat as instructed and wait for Dad to come in. My hands shake so bad that even squeezing them doesn't quell them. The echo of a door snapping open and the grating of metal legs against the concrete floor draws my attention. I look up into the face of my father, weathered and older than the one I remember. His wavy black hair is peppered with grey, and his face is covered by a thick beard, which I don't like. It's not my dad's face. This is not the man I know and love.

"Sugar bear?" he whispers, and the disbelief in his eyes cracks my soul. He might not look the same, he might be wafer thin, but his voice brings all my emotions rushing to the surface.

"Dad," I choke out, putting my hand to the glass.

He places his fingers against mine, and I know he wants to touch me. I want to touch and hug him too. I'm so sorry for the mess I caused.

"I can't believe it. Harry sent me the message." He shakes his head, his lips push together to keep the tears from falling. My dad never let me see him cry, but this man is different—broken of spirit. "I didn't think you'd come. You said to stop sending you cards. That I was no longer your father—"

The pain forces my eyes shut. "I said that." My voice is so hushed I hope he can hear me. "I kept the last birthday card you sent me in my school locker."

His smile lights up his face as if I had given him the top prize. "Oh Lara, I'm glad. So glad." It seems he's seeing me for the first time, his eyes studying all aspects of me. "You're beautiful. Look like your mom." He chews on a finger. "I don't know what to say. I don't know what it's like to have a grown daughter. I'm sorry."

"It's not your fault. I just wanted to see you." He nods in a slow, controlled way.

I feel my presence is making him anxious, that he wants me to go away again. Why does everything have to be so hard? Can't it go back to how it used to be?

"I'm not allowed to ask about your mom, but I hope she's well. You guys still happy with what's his name?"

My mind flashes to Jax's smiling face while we sit across from each other over a Monopoly board. I nod to Dad, wiping goo from my nose. "Sure. Never better, I guess. I have a younger sister, a brother."

Dad nods. "I heard about that a few years ago. Your Mom told me."

Bells go off in my head. "Mom comes to see you?"

Dad runs a hand through his hair. "No, nothing like that. Sometimes she would send a letter through her attorney. Nothing personal, and nothing from her. Just news."

He means threats. They've threatened him to stop trying to get in touch with us. We've moved on. There is nothing left for him with his old family.

"So, how's school?" Dad asks with a laugh.

I try to smile. "Pretty good. I get good grades, have friends. Home life is okay. Mom works a lot." I twist my lip, chewing the inside of my cheek. I know the questions I need to ask, but I don't want to blurt them out.

He avoids my references to home life. "You have a boyfriend?"

"Did. I dumped him yesterday. He was a creep. After only one thing, like most guys, I guess."

Dad nods. "Good for you. School right now is most important. Keep at it."

"I will. How are you?"

Dad shakes his head with a bitter sigh. He leans back in his chair and crosses his arms. The distance between us multiplies, and I sense his reluctance to share with me. "Tonight is mac and cheese night, and I am starting a new book from the library, so I guess everything's swell."

Swell. Have I ever heard Dad say that before? Though mac and cheese was his favorite meal, especially Kraft instant dinner.

"I read about what happened, with the parole and the stabbing. I'm sorry." I take a deep breath and swallow, but my throat is as dry as sandpaper.

His face flashes surprise.

"I use the computer at the library. They try to protect me from everything, but I don't let them."

Dad shifts in his seat as if he's going to erupt with the question on his lips. "Lara." He leans forward with his elbow on the counter between us. "Why are you here?"

"I need you to tell me what happened. Fill in the blanks," I whisper, glancing over my shoulder to make sure the guards aren't loitering around too closely. "Someone shot at Mom, but I know you didn't send them. So what happened after that?"

Dad's eyes flash with anger. "Why would you believe in me after all these years?"

"Dad." My eyes soften and grow wet as anger and spite fills his face. "There isn't time to explain. I need to know. I deserve the truth, don't I? You're my father, and I want to know why you're in here."

"Who sent you? Who put you up to this?"

"No. One." I meet his eyes, imploring him to believe in me, but as he pushes back his chair, I sense he's further away than ever. He thinks I'm a traitor? I am a stranger, even if his blood does run in my veins.

"I can't talk about this. Not with you. Sorry." Dad tilts his head back. "Guard!"

"No," I hiss and lean forward. "Daddy, what was Mom doing at the time agency before she died?"

I blurt it out without thinking and want to fade away and die. Dad holds up his arm to the guard to give him more time. Great job, I've managed to spill my secret to two people now. I may as well take a bulletin out in the paper. I feel nothing but self-loathing for what I've done to Dad, Mom, and the world.

"Lara," he says softly, "why did you say *died*?"

"I slipped," I say as I lift my tear-ridden face off the table. "I meant … shot at."

"No, no, you didn't." Dad shakes his head slowly. "When they brought you to see me on your seventh birthday, what did I say to you?"

My mouth falls open at the test. My eyes flitter about as I try to force a memory I don't have. I blink and take a deep breath, allowing my chest to rise. I see dancing flame across a layer of icing, but I have no idea what year the image is from, and I see no faces. At this important time, I can't draw a memory to save my life.

I have to try, but I have nothing. I decide to throw out my best guess and hope it is the right answer. "That we'd be together one day."

His shoulders relax, and he uncrosses his arms. "And how'd you react?"

Thinking back, a trail of blood oozes from my nose. I grab a tissue from my bag and use it to pinch my nose.

My mind transports me back to being a scared little girl, crying into my pillow, begging for my dad. I can't sleep. No one can because of my night terrors. Jax is sitting beside me to calm me down, but I thrash, scratching him with my fingernails as deep as I can, wishing he'd go away.

"I cried." My voice is hollow. "I had tantrums. Mom decided ..." Tears stream down my face. "... seeing you was too traumatic for me. That's when they cut you out."

Dad nods, his lips blubbering. "Guess there isn't much to say, is there?"

"Except for what Mom was working on. I need to know."

"Why?" he asks, wearing the question on his face.

"Just humor me. Please, this once."

He stares at me. I try to push him in the right direction by adding, "Dad. Please." My eyes are wide, pleading, and my mind wills him to answer.

After what feels an eternity, he nods. "She landed a big contract and went to work for Rewind. She worked in R&D. In those days, time travel was barely understood and not for regular folks."

"She's a scientist, then?"

Dad nods. "She was working on some improvements to the time travel device, something that would allow parties to interact with the past without dying or going insane. She always said that effect was a bug in the system. It shouldn't happen. She's been trying to fix it for as long as I can remember."

The implications are huge. "So anyone could change the past?"

"Only certain ones with higher privileges. Or something."

"Did she ever finish?"

Dad shrugs. "I'm not big on current events. She's your mom. Why don't you ask her?"

I decide that's exactly what I need to do. "I heard on the news you were hurt."

His eyes cloud over, and he pushes his chair back. "I can't talk to you about this. Sorry, Lara."

"Dad." I sigh, intending to plead my case, but he signals for the guards.

Our conversation is over.

When they come for him, I do my best to keep a smile on my face. His hands are shackled together, and a chain runs down to his feet. He's being treated like a terrorist instead of someone that failed at murdering his wife. I watch them escort him out of the room. There's no way we're done. I have to come back. I still have questions I need him to answer.

I ask the lawyer to take me to see my mom. He drops me off at the door, and I enter the sterile hall. The place seems to be a typical office building. Receptionists at the front type on their keyboards, and the desks are made of polished mahogany. Behind them, a giant clock's minute hand spins backwards.

Music chirps like songbirds in the background, and off to the side is a waterfall, where children gather to throw coins for making wishes. Across from that is a waiting area filled with magazines and books, where people fill out questionnaires.

I bypass all of that and go straight to the elevators. No one bats an eye. They must have seen me before. I check the directory by the doors and see she's on the top floor. My finger slams the up arrow, and I wait for the chime. Stepping inside, I hit the button for the top floor and wait for the stainless steel doors to slide shut. The elevator jerks beneath me as it begins its upward crawl, and I spend the moments trying to decide how I am going to play this. How will I get the information I need to know, and what is Mom going to do about it?

The elevator dings, and two men in lab coats step inside. They are too busy talking to notice me. One of them makes sweeping gestures with his hand. "What are we going to do about this?"

The other man shrugs. "What can we do? We need to extract those memories from Jenkins. He truly believes he spent the last five years in prison. His personality, everything about him has completely changed."

"He needs to be kept locked up."

"He is locked up," the man says hotly. "This is Montgomery's mess. She needs to clean it up."

My mom? My posture turns rigid.

"If the board figures out what we did …We are supposed to store memories. Store, not swap them around. How the hell did this happen?"

"It's a kink. It'll get worked out."

"Yeah, except now the man is jumping through time with no way to stop. What if he finds us? What if he kills us?"

I can't believe what I'm hearing or that they are talking about it in front of me. They are so worked up, they probably don't even realize I'm here. If they are saying what I think they are, my mother created a serial killer and gave him the ability to leap through time off the grid so Rewind and the government couldn't keep track of it.

That had all sorts of illegal written all over it. And stupid.

The man snorts as the elevator stops. "She did it on purpose. I know it. And somehow I have to prove it."

"At least he's in a coma. Thank God we were able to get that syringe before he leaped again."

"If we can keep him that way."

"If."

When the door opens, they leave and I go up the remaining floor by myself. I step out onto plush carpet. The walls are made of glass, and I am able to see into the conference rooms that line the hallway. The offices inside are small, with no windows and white doors. I study all the name plates until I find one with my mother's name. Taking a deep, shaking breath I turn the door knob and push it open.

Mom is bent over her computer, holding a phone to her ear. Her curled hair looks more tussled than ever, and she's grabbing at it. She looks totally stressed out.

"I'm on my way to the lab. Don't do anything until I get there." She hangs up the phone and looks up. The lines on her face increase tenfold. "Lara?"

I step inside and close the door. "Sounds like you're busy."

She rushes over to me and places a wrist on my forehead. "Are you sick again? What's the matter, honey? Why aren't you in school?"

"I needed to see you. I miss you, Mom." My chin quivers, and I chastise myself for being so emotional, but I didn't break time travel law so she could work on some new feature for a stupid company.

She gives me a sad smile and cradles my chin, giving it kisses. "Well, this is a first." She hugs me, a good warm one, and I am crushed in the strength of her embrace. "I never thought I'd hear you say that again, you know that?"

Resting my head on her shoulder, I want to tell her everything, but it's too soon. "Maybe we can go for lunch?"

Mom sighs. "Oh, honey. I have so much to do, and there's a crisis in the lab."

"I went to see him," I say in anger, almost to punish her for putting her work first. "I went to see Dad. In jail," I add, in case she didn't get where I was coming from.

She did.

Her eyes light up like circles of fire. "Lara Montgomery—"

"Crane."

Her passion has fueled mine, and my temper begins to sizzle, but she isn't backing down. She places her hands on her hips and paces.

"And what, he said something to you that upset you?"

I shake my head. "Just the opposite. He was nice, but … like a stranger. I need to know, do you really believe he did it? Really?"

"He was convicted," she spits out. She must hate that I'm making her talk about it.

"Innocent people get convicted, especially if they're set up."

Mom rolls her eyes. "Lara, don't tell me you've been on the Internet again. I told you he'll say anything. Anything, if it means getting out of prison."

"I think there's truth in what he says. I know he didn't do it, Mom. I know."

"How?" Her question is practically a dare. "Tell me how you know."

I stammer and struggle. I know the answer I want to give her.

"Because he's your father," she whispers. "I know you will never give this up, but there's nothing we can do, Lara. What's done is done. Your father is guilty, as much as you hate to see it."

My heart palpitates, and I draw a breath. "Why didn't you stick by him? Why?"

"He tried to kill me."

My jaw is set tight. "You ripped me away from him. I remember it."

Mom's eyes spill tears. "Is that all you remember? Is it? Do you remember the horrible apartments we lived in? The horror we went through those first months. The trial? You think I wanted that for you, for me? Don't be insane, Lara. If your father was innocent, they wouldn't have found the gun at our apartment."

"It was planted."

She snickers with bitterness. "You sound like him. I'll be damned if you'll go see him again!"

My fist pounds my chest. "I'm a Crane! His blood is in me, so you can't tell me what to do!"

I turn to pull the door open, but she grabs my wrist, spins me around, and slaps me right across the cheek. Shocked, my mouth drops open, and I cover the sting with the palm of my hand. Rather than apologize, she breathes with indignation, her top lip curled onto her bottom.

"We are Montgomerys now. Everything we have, everything we love, comes from this life."

"You really are ashamed you were a Crane once, aren't you?" I whisper, realizing the horror of the truth Lara wrote in her diary. "I'm a sick reminder that you loved John once. That we had this life together in a rundown apartment." I take a deep breath, my own words cutting me.

"Is that really what you think?" she says, face full of distress. "You think I hate you?"

"Maybe." My nostrils flare. "Last month you didn't come to my dance recital. Last week you skipped our usual breakfast." Where are these resentments coming from?

"Work." Her eyes are sad and she frowns.

"Screw work!" I scream. "Work isn't what's important. Do you know what is? I am! Mike and Molly are important. We talked about getting you a gift, and you know what they wanted to get you? Gift certificates for spas because they know how stressed out you are all the time. They have nannies when they should have you."

"I feel guilty enough. I don't need you adding to it, Lara."

"You should feel guilty." My lips curl in a snarl. I can't believe I traded my dad for this woman. I should've left her in the alley to die.

Suddenly, I'm crying. My shoulders are heaving, and the sobs can barely escape my lungs, fighting for freedom. I cover my eyes and nearly rub them straight off with the heels of my hands. I hate myself and wish the world would swallow me whole.

Mom's arms wrap around me in the biggest of bear hugs. She pulls me down into the sofa beside her. I am like a little girl in her arms as she sways in time with me. "It was so much easier when you were little."

I laugh through the hurt. "I want to be with you. I wish I was enough."

"Oh, Lara." Her voice sounds broken, and I see the strain on her face. Her eyes gaze off into the distance at the bookcases lining her office walls. "Let me go to the lab, fix a few things, then I'll take you to lunch."

"Your work—"

"Will still be here tonight." Mom smiles. "It's not a lot, but it's all I can give right now, while I finish this thing." She kisses my forehead as I nod, then rushes from the office, and for a moment I sit and listen to the air conditioner kick in.

I stand and march to her desk. Sitting in the rolling chair, I rifle through her drawers. I can't find anything of note, but I do find some pictures. On top is a wedding picture of her and Jax. Below that I find ones of me and the kids, which should make me smile but doesn't.

The center drawer is locked, so I move on to the computer. A quick shake of the mouse clears the screen saver. I peer over at the door to make sure no one is there before I type in a password I think she might use—my birthday—but it doesn't work.

I sigh and as a last ditch effort type in Dad's birthday. The computer dings, and the screen saver fades. I am brought to a perfectly neat blue desktop where the few icons are lined up on the side, but several applications are minimized to the taskbar, which excites me.

First, I click on her open email, and my eyes spot a chain letter, a picture of kittens, and the usual joke email. So much for working hard. But the next program I see contains a report she was drafting. A Rewind watermark is stamped *Confidential*.

No one is coming yet, so I read.

The events of this week are regrettable but unavoidable as we move into the human testing part of the program. Mr. Jenkins' family has my deepest sympathies, but we have made great strides towards the possibility of time travel longer than fifteen minutes. For the right candidate, the natural time travel ability will be unlocked.

Mr. Jenkins remained in the past for twenty minutes, and once he returned we "removed some key memories" of his life and "inserted new ones." He was adamant that these memories actually happened. He became hostile and aggressive when we suggested otherwise. As far as he knew, he'd had these memories for years.

Think of the advantages this would have against murderers, terrorists, and pedophiles. We could change who people are at the core level and by partnering with law enforcement, reshape the world.

Mr. Jenkins returned to the past ten times. With medicine and treatment, we tried to help him through the headaches and brain hemorrhaging. First, the fresh memories assaulted him in the present. When those tapered off, the nose bleeds started. After that, his decent into madness quickened as his uncontrollable ability to jump through time grew stronger. He grew increasingly confused and forgetful with each trip.

His actions were proving dangerous, so we put him into a drug-induced coma. I will declare him brain dead tomorrow and have him taken off life support.

While this information appears to be dire, he was hooked up to our equipment for the duration. While our methods may be questioned, our loyalties to the program can't. I hope once you examine his scans you'll see we have enough data to move forward on a new approach.

My closest assistant, Delilah, continues to flag customers whose brain scans say they may be able to survive a full time-travel merge. Once we can convince them to join the program, we will have more test subjects, and once we nail down this issue, we can move toward our two long-term goals.

Patricia, I know I am asking for more time, and you need this done ASAP. Please see I am working on this as hard as I can.

No one wants this to work more than I do.

My nose has been bleeding since yesterday.

I scroll down and see the intended recipient of the email—Senator Patricia James. It is all coming together, and I am terrified what it means. Mom is up to her eyeballs in illegal research that is killing people. And her assistant Delilah was my technician in my version of the past. I wish I could leap there and find out what she knows, but maybe I can do the next best thing. Maybe I can question her now.

As I'm leaving the office, I bump into Mom. She gasps with surprise. "Where are you off to in such a hurry?"

"Bathroom. Meet you in the lobby in ten minutes?"

Mom nods. "See you then."

I sprint toward the bathroom. I only hope I can get this done in time.

Chapter Ten

I knock on Delilah's office door and push it open. I smell her afternoon orange tea, and a warm glow emanates from the lit candle on her desk. She spins in her office chair.

"Yes? Lara! What a nice surprise. I didn't know you were visiting."

I smile and enter her small office. The desk is cluttered, and she looks very busy, so I need to be brief.

"Having lunch with Mom and thought I'd say hi." I take the seat in front of her desk. "She had to spring out to the lab. A big emergency."

Delilah's eyes cloud over. "Yes." She returns to her computer and her shoulders hunch with the weight of the world.

I shake my head. "I can't believe it. Time traveling without use of the system? Off the grid? I guess that would give Senator James a lot of power, huh?"

Delilah's head snaps up. She's perspiring, and her lips twitch at the corners. "She...she told you?"

I nod. "But I won't tell anyone." I hold up a hand. "Scout's honor."

Anger flickers across her face. "Why in the world she would … This is dangerous, understand? We could all go to jail. All of us. Even the Senator. You can't breathe a word of it. Promise me, Lara."

I nod. "I never realized you were so important, flagging people down with this power. How do you do it?"

"Really, Lara ..." She glances over her shoulder. "We study the brain waves. We can detect when someone tries to interfere with the past, even by accident. Then I can just mark their chart."

"And make sure they keep coming back?" I ask.

Delilah nods quickly. "I keep them under close surveillance. I can see when their brain is changing. After that, I make sure they keep wanting to change things."

I cock an eyebrow. "And you make sure no one realizes they are changing things."

Her eyes grow sharp. "But you can't tell anyone. If the police, the government, were to find out we're working for the senator, we'd all fry. What we're doing breaks all the time travel laws Congress put in place."

Forcing a smile, I stand. "I promise," I say, my mouth growing dry.

I ponder all the times I traveled into the past to map out my route. Each time, Delilah was my assistant. Was it mere chance, or is it possible she was spying on me? She had been my mom's partner. Is it possible she continued the research after my mom died?

But if Delilah was keeping tabs on me, if she was monitoring my brain when I changed the past, that means she witnessed it. And if she kept it a secret, that means she flagged me. And if she flagged me, I soon could end up like Mr. Jenkins.

Chapter Eleven

All through lunch I try to enjoy my time with Mom, but my mind keeps drifting away. Rewind is set up to be an indulgent service, like getting your butt lipo-sucked or getting a massage. It's supposed to be fun, but apparently it's a cover for something deeper and more dangerous. My mom, the woman I've missed all my life, is working on something that could change the course of history for the better or the worse. I know how badly changing one little thing messed up my life, my dad's life.

How dangerous would the power to remove memories be? Memories make us who we are, that much I've learned. What if Democrats assassinate the next Republican president before he is even old enough to walk? What if they learn how to wipe out memories on a mass scale and use it to control the population?

I thought Mom was mugged and killed. I thought she was innocent, but now I'm finding out there were reasons people could have wanted her dead, wanted her research stopped. Mom was supposed to be special, angelic, and I was supposed to be special too. When I first discovered I could interact with the past, I thought I was the only one.

My mind drifts back to that day. The first day I traveled back in time. Back on my sixteenth birthday when I went back to my very first birthday.

****

I'm sitting in the corner of a family-style restaurant with an alternating-color tile floor. The room is decorated with pink balloons and streamers. Apparently, I'm in the midst of a party. A woman with curly hair holds a baby girl wearin a pink headband. Around them people are smiling, even though the baby is still crying from the popped balloons.

One of them says 'Happy 1st Birthday'

I'm confused and frustrated. Why am I here? Who are these people? Was I invited to the party, and if so, why didn't I bring a present? Glancing down in my hand, I see a crumpled flier. I smooth it in my hand and see it's from Rewind.

You may experience temporary short-term memory loss. You have fifteen minutes in the past.

In the past?

Time travel?

I look up at the woman in front of me. The curly hair framing her face reminds me of mine. She's bouncing her baby girl on her leg, and I realize it's not a newborn but an older baby. The woman kisses the baby's cheek, her eyes twinkling like stars.

"Lara, it's just a balloon. It's okay."

Lara?

A young man I assume is the father sits next to her. He dances a doll in front of the baby's chunky arms a giant grin on his face. The baby giggles and reaches for it.

"You always know what to do," the woman says.

He winks at her. "It's why you married me."

"One of the reasons." They lean forward to kiss.

Their love radiates around them like a glowing bubble, and for a little while I'm inside it, taking in the sight of the couple kissing the baby, laughing with each other. I forget I don't belong here as they cut the cake and the baby smashes it with her fists. I love the way the dad drapes his arm over his wife's shoulder.

I take in one final moment of watching the mom cuddle the baby before I turn away and smack into the waitress behind me holding a drink tray. Squealing in horror, I bend down to help her. Water and soda is splashed on the floor, all over my sneaker, everywhere.

"I'm so sorry," I say, helping her pick up the broken glass and placing it on her tray.

"It's okay," she mumbles, but I know it isn't. Her cheeks are bright red; she's mad.

A flash of memory hits me from my time at Rewind. *"You will be like a hologram, unable to touch or interact with the past, even though they will see you. After you are gone, you will fade from their memory, and it will be as if you were never there."*

But I bumped into the waitress. I picked up the glass.

"I can interact with the past," I whisper as the gears in my mind begin to whirl.

Beginning to form a plan, I throw a glance over my shoulder at the parents as my world fades to black.

****

I come to awareness as I'm stabbing the prongs of my fork into a Cobb salad. I sigh. It's one of my favorite lunches, but I can't focus on eating it. I look up. Apparently I'm still at lunch with my mom.

She stops chewing and sips her iced tea. "For someone who wanted to go to lunch, you're not doing a very good job of actually eating it."

"Sorry." I cringe and sip my drink too. "I feel real bad how I yelled at you earlier."

Mom smiles, not altogether happy but not pissed off either. "I'm sorry too. I shouldn't have slapped you, and I feel real bad about that. Real bad." She uses her baby blue cotton napkin to wipe her mouth. "I promised myself it would never happen again, and here we both are."

"Again?" Her words haunt me. Why did she slap me the last time? Is our relationship that bad?

"It'll be different this time." Mom nods and digs back into her sandwich.

My mind wanders back to the fight in the kitchen I overheard. "How are things with the senator?"

The lines on her face become serious. "We haven't spoken in a while. We don't talk all the time, you know."

"Oh," is all I can bother to say.

"It's true we used to be closer." It seems Mom can easily spin a web of lies, leaving me to wonder what else she might be lying about. "She gave me my job, my career. I have a lot to thank her for."

"She's one of the founders of Rewind," I say, trying to make it sound less of a question than it really is.

Mom nods. "Without her we never would've met Jax, and I wouldn't have this job. We owe her ... a lot."

My stomach rolls.

"Why the sudden interest in Donovan's mom?"

I shrug. "No reason. Just figured I'd ask." I take a moment to swallow some water. "Have you ever seen a gold dragon tattoo before?"

Mom chokes and spits out her iced tea all over her plate. She reaches for her napkin to cover her mouth, eyes wide.

I am going to take that for a yes.

"Lara, where have you seen a man with a dragon tattoo?"

"Oh, I don't know. Around. On the subway, I think." I try to play it casual and coil a piece of hair around a finger.

"Well ... keep your distance. Those men aren't friendly."

"So you know who they are?"

Mom nods. "Only from what I read in the papers. They're with the mob."

Now it's my turn to be shocked. "The mob?"

Why would the mob be following me? What was I getting myself into?

"Yes, so keep your distance."

I nod. "Promise."

"Good." She pauses, and the tension increases between us. "So what did you and your dad talk about?"

"Dad?" I ask with a mouth full of salad. I take the time to chew before swallowing. "Oh you know. Grades. Asked about my boyfriend."

Mom smirks. "I bet he loved that."

"Well, what else is there to talk about?" I fish through my salad looking for the last crouton. "You met Dad in high school, didn't you?"

Mom has a faraway stare on her face, one I've never. "He was a football player, not the star, except maybe to me. We were friendly." Mom shrugs, twirling her hair around her finger. "We hung in groups back then, and he asked me to go to the movies alone. And that was that."

She smiles wide at the memory, and I swear her cheeks are flushed. I guess her memory of John Crane can't be all bad.

"We married young, and he supported me all through college even when his career took a hit. I never would've guessed …" Her voice cracks. "… would've guessed where we'd end up." She returns her attention to her sandwich.

I've been so focused on how I felt and what happened to Dad that I haven't stopped to think until now how hard it must have been on Mom to think Dad wanted her dead. But it wasn't real, it was a lie. It didn't matter to Mom, though, because to her it was real.

My head is suddenly jolted with pain. My eyes squeeze shut, and I see a flash of light. The freight train of a memory is back to make its run through my brain. I try to keep it away, concentrating only on the present, but it's coming hard and fast. I only hope that this time I won't fall on the ground with my nose bleeding.

****

When the flash of light clears, I'm a little girl lying in the spare bedroom of my grandmother's house. The comforter is pink with lace trim, perfect for a little girl, and the room has all of my things, but I'm still scared. Each breath I take is loud in my ears, and all I want to do is pretend to sleep.

I bury my nose in my pillow and squeeze my arm tight against my stuffed unicorn, the one doll I could never live without. My breathing slows, and I shut my eyes until they're barely open, so it looks as if I've fallen asleep because I'm not alone. Mom is on her knees by my bed, stroking my curls and humming a song. "Twinkle Little Star," I think. It's hard to tell because her voice is quivering. It scares me that Mommy could be so upset she can't hum our song. A sob catches in her throat, and I pretend to sleep, so she'll think I'm okay too. But my heart is broken in ways I can't understand.

I miss Daddy. I want him back, and I don't understand why the news and all the adults think he'd hurt Mommy or me. He loves us. But I want Mom to know I'm okay. I want her to know I'm going to be okay.

"Come have some tea, Miranda."

My grandmother's voice nearly makes me jump, but I manage to keep myself together as Mom pulls her hand away from my head. She pulls the blanket around my small frame, making me feel cozy, safe. She covers my forehead in little kisses, and I can't help but smile. About the time I think she's going to leave, I hear her speak.

"How can I …?" Her voice warbles into a sob, and my grandmother's heels make their way across the floor.

"Come," she whispers. "We will drink tea, and you will pull yourself together."

"John—"

"Tonight, you cry," my grandmother says, "and I'll cry too, but tomorrow Lara needs us. She needs you. You need to be stronger than this. Tomorrow."

****

The sun seems brighter when I reopen my eyes again. I rub my forehead, and Mom stares at me. "Lara? Are you all right?"

"Just a headache," I say and rush some iced tea.

She takes a deep breath and struggles to release it. "I'm calling your doctor when I get back to the office. I hope we can get in to see him in a few days."

"Okay," I say while my stomach sinks. I don't know if the doctor will give me a clean bill of health, but I really don't want to go, and I'm pretty sure after my bleeding nose last night, I'm not going to get out of it.

"Okay? I thought you hated going to the doctor?"

I shrug. "Can you drop me off at the house? I have homework and stuff. When you're done."

"Sure," she says and checks her watch. "I guess it is time to get back to work, but I had fun, Lara. Really. Let's do this again, real soon." She takes a moment to give me a brilliant smile and then holds her hand up to get our waiter's attention.

I try to be happy but can't. I'm a ticking time bomb.

****

Mom drops me off at the door and apologizes for having to work late again tonight but promises to come to the doctor with me in the morning. I rush up the steps snoop around. Only one room has a closed door. When I peek inside, I see a few nice pieces of furniture, one of them a desk with a computer on top.

Bingo.

Stepping in, I close the door behind me and sit behind the desk. Thanks to knowing my dad's birthday, I get in the computer easily. Note to Mom, you really need to diversify your passwords.

A check of her email shows the same results as before, and with a quick system scan, I find her confidential files— system schematics for memory storage, extraction, and drawings I can't even begin to understand. They seem to be a bunch of molecules and atoms drawn out in some drafting program. The only label I see is the name *John*. Must be code for something, but why use Dad's name if she thinks he tried to kill her? Maybe Mom was pining for a life lost.

I'm about to leave when my search for *Patricia* finally returns a file folder buried in the system. The name *Archive* catches my attention. Mom went to great lengths to hide it from the casual searcher. Opening the file, I find a string of documents with an assortment of dates. None of the file names are red flags to me, so I'll have to go through them one at a time. Starting with the oldest seems like the best idea. I organize by date and am surprised how far back they go.

Ten years.

I open what turns out to be an email, and my breath catches in my throat. It is dated exactly two weeks before Mom's attempted murder.

Or her actual death.

Patricia;

You've been a dear friend for so long. It pains me to write this letter to you. I respectfully, and with a heavy heart, must hand in my resignation.

Lara is still so young. John and I have been fighting more. I have promised to give our marriage one more chance. And to honestly do that, I am going to need to take a step back in my career.

I hope you achieve everything we've brainstormed all those late nights. I know how important it is to you and the world to find an end to violence.

I'll make sure my current contract is completed, but after that I will be moving on. Thank you for everything you've done for me over these last few years.

Miranda Crane

I sit and stare at the screen as if doing so will get it to leap up at me and explain what this all means. Mom was ready to leave Rewind two weeks before her death. Two weeks! That couldn't have been a coincidence. What if they didn't want to let her go? What if she knew things she shouldn't, and the only way to deal with that fact was to make sure she never talked about them, and then, when their assassination attempt fell through, they framed my dad?

Is it too far of a stretch? Was the senator, Donovan's mom, actually capable of murder?

I need to find out more about this woman, but quietly. I don't want to spook her or Donovan. There is no way I can afford for them to realize I'm onto them. She's a United States senator for goodness' sake. If I'm wrong, I will burn.

But if I'm right … God, if I'm right it's going to take more than a few emails to prove it. Still, they are all I have, so I continue exploring them. Perhaps Mom is keeping this folder in case she needs leverage against Patricia James? I doubt she realizes how dangerous the woman is.

Senator;

Clearly their relationship wasn't as chummy as it used to be, but why? What happened between them to cause a rift, and if there is a rift, why is Mom still secretly working for her?

Senator;
My assistant Delilah continues to use the memory program to find candidates for the John project. We are only a few months away from human testing.

The next one:

Miranda,
Start human testing immediately or I'll find someone who will.

The memory program was a cover for the John program. I assume now that unlocking the brain's ability to time travel off the grid, away from police scrutiny, is the John project, and the memory storage program is nothing but a cover for their research. A way to find participants. Humans are nothing more than guinea pigs to these people. The senator was clearly upset with Mom, but why? Was Mom becoming resistant to the work? She wanted out once. Is it possible she wanted out again?

Another email from only a few weeks ago. The subject is simply *You?* It contains an attachment of a news article from Reuters.

"REPORTER FOUND DEAD"

After asking questions about Rewind's ethics, Joyce Meyers, an investigative reporter, was found dead of an apparent suicide in her bathtub late last night. Calls from her neighbors alerted the police to screams heard earlier that day, and they worried for her safety.

Ms. Meyers, famous for asking probing questions of Rewind Lead Scientist Miranda Montgomery at a press conference last week, defended herself by saying she had a source who had proof that Rewind was conducting illegal research. She refused to give up her source when asked, saying to do so would put her source's life in harm's way.

A suicide note was found at the scene and a police investigation is currently ongoing.

Who was her source? Mom?

It's clear Mom thinks Senator James is capable of murder, practically accusing her of it in her email. Whatever is going on, I need to find out more about Joyce and the senator.

My head rages with pain, and my hands flutter to my temples. I grunt, feeling the onslaught of another memory barreling toward me. When we collide, my eyes snap open, and I grip the edges of the desk. The memory floods me.

****

I'm sitting at the same desk, only my dress is short and my hair straight. My hand is using the mouse, moving all the confidential system files over to an empty folder— systems, theories, blueprints. Plus the science behind what Mom is trying to do the human mind. As the files are copied, I glance over my shoulder to make sure no one is coming. I'm on edge, nervous.

I find a video in the archive folder I didn't see before. Clicking play, Mom's face comes into focus. She appears nervous, scared, and when she speaks, her words chill my heart.

"If I have an accident, if I end up dead, let this serve as proof that Senator Patricia James, my colleague and old friend, had a hand in it." Her hands shake as she wipes a strand of hair from her face. "I dare not let on that I know how dangerous she's become, but I am going to finish my current project and then, God help me, take my family and get out of the country. Hide. If I live that long."

Mom blinks back tears. "Jax, Lara, no one knows how scared I've been the last few months, and I have to keep it that way or put their lives in jeopardy." She takes a deep breath. "I never should've listened to Patricia. Never."

She goes on to recant what I've already deduced—the memory program is nothing but a cover. The senator convinced her to start illegal testing on a project hidden from the US government. She wants the technology for herself, to improve the country and put herself in power.

"I used to have the same goals." She swallows hard. "But I wanted it to help people like my Lara. Like myself. Victims. Patricia wants it for herself, and that can't be allowed. So once I'm done and safely out of the country, I'll send this video and be done with her once and for all."

The video ends there, and I sit for a moment, unable to believe what I've heard. My investigation into Dad's conviction had unearthed information I hadn't suspected, and now I'm caught up in something dangerous, something I can't handle on my own. But what choice do I have? If I tell Donovan, I might lose him forever, and going to the police might get Mom, Jax, or Dad killed. I have no choice.

I copy the video over and pull a small flash drive out from the side of the computer once it's done. That's it. It's time.

Time to deliver the evidence.

****

My eyes open as the memory fades.

Was I Joyce Meyer's source? Did I get her killed.

If so, did Lara know that? And why was she snooping in Mom's office in the first place? I have a reason. What was her reason?

I need to find out.

The front doorbell rings, stopping me in my tracks. I make sure everything appears as I found it then rush to the door. It chimes again rapid fire, as if someone fell asleep on a church organ. My spirits lift when I see Rick on the other side.

"Rick," I say with surprise.

He wears a slight smile and peers over my shoulder into the foyer. "Wow, looks pretty fancy in there."

I blush and laugh out of nerves. "Well, you know ... ahem ... I'm surprised to see you here."

"Not as surprised as I am," Rick admits. "When you weren't in school, I knew something might be wrong. Or, you know, you might need notes for Mr. Johnson's history class. I have it third period, and I know you're in the fifth."

So he kept tabs on my schedule. "Thanks. That's real nice of you. Sure, I'd love some notes."

I step aside and let him in, making sure I secure the front door before I lead him into the living room. He looks around the place as he perches himself on the edge of the sofa.

"Sofa's don't bite," I say with a smirk.

"Huh? Oh." He chortles and sits back. "Sorry. I feel like I'm dirtying the place by being here."

"You're not." I pause and bite the inside of my cheek. "Want a drink? I mean juice, soda. Oh, bite me."

He stares at me for a moment, and we both burst out laughing. Fishing inside his bag, he pulls out a few sheets of paper and hands them to me.

"Wow." My eyebrows rise. "I'm surprised there are actual notes. Here I thought they might be an excuse. To come in."

Rick smirks. "You caught me. Guess I wanted to see how things were with your dad and everything."

I shrug and shake my head. "I saw him, and it led to more questions than answers, and he acted like ... I was a stranger." I bite the inside of my lip. "Guess I am. Here. Hell, I'm even a stranger to myself."

"Sorry. Has to be rough."

"Like sandpaper." I tuck my hair behind my ears. "I found a key hidden in the back of my wallet, but I don't know what it opens."

"Can I see?"

Fishing it out of my purse, I hand it to him. He turns it over and holds it up to inspect. "Looks like the one I used to carry for my locker at the Y. I don't know why you'd go there, though."

Maybe because I didn't want anyone to see what I put in it. I take the key back and study it again, noticing *63* is engraved in the center. My mind flashes to white.

I glance fearfully over my shoulder before shoving a blue duffle bag inside and locking the door. I hurry, nearly running, to get to the pool before anyone sees me.

I'm back with Rick again. Why was I so afraid? Is it all related to the senator and the death of the reporter Joyce Meyers? It's time to find out.

"Anything else?" Rick asks.

I shrug. "I might be on to something."

"Oh?" He sits up straighter.

I lean forward to tell him about what I found, but then the front door slams. "We're home!"

"My sister and brother," I explain. "I'm in here!" I bellow.

They stop in their tracks at seeing Rick. Mike's face is untrusting, his lips drawn together in a line, while Molly smiles shyly.

"This is Rick, an old friend."

"Are we still going to the mall?" Molly asks.

"Oh, sorry." Rick stands up. "I didn't realize you had plans."

"No, it's okay. I'm glad you came by." I stand up, glancing between the kids and Rick. "Why don't you come with us? We're going to take the T and then get dinner. It might be fun. Right?"

I turn to the kids, who seem unsure, but then they nod. Expectantly, I face Rick and tug anxiously on my fingers. "Come on, it's a free meal."

"I'll come, but I won't take your money. I'm not a pity case."

My face falls. "I know that. I was just trying to be nice."

He bends down to the kids and winks at them. "Last one to the curb is a rotten egg!"

He takes off running, and the kids chase after him, but I remain in place for a moment. I can't shake the feeling that Rick is different, that he isn't the boy I knew, but I shake it off as nerves and run after them.

"Wait for me guys!"

Chapter Twelve

All the way to the mall, Rick engages the kids, and I watch as they open up to him—Molly with her wide eyes and Mike with his science jokes. I can't shake the feeling that something about him is different. Maybe it's nothing, and I'm on edge because of my growing feelings for Donovan. Maybe I'm looking for reasons I can't be with Rick.

I buy the kids the Happy Meals they want, and after everyone eats we head to the jewelry store. We let the kids wander ahead but only far enough to enjoy a little freedom. As we walk I read the sale signs, and when Rick suddenly takes my hand with his clammy palm, I jump at the unexpected affection.

He bites his lip, and his eyes look like a wounded puppy's. "Is this something you don't want?"

"No, I—" I don't know what I'm feeling. "I wasn't expecting it. We can't let the kids see." I pull my hand back, and there's no mistaking the disappointment on Rick's face.

He falls quiet. I want to explain, but first I have a necklace to pick out and birthstones to order. I pay with my credit card and accept the receipt, so we can pick up the purchase in a week. I wonder what will happen between now and then, but I manage a smile and drop the receipt into my purse.

Molly talks about dresses, and Mike talks about sports on the way through the mall toward the entrance. They pause when we stop to let them ride the carousel. They are so excited and have such giant grins on their faces that I can't help but feel better.

"Look at me, Lara!" Molly giggles, holding her arms over her head.

I take out my phone and snap a picture before I turn to Rick. "I'm sorry about earlier. I like holding hands with you. Things are complicated."

"You think I don't know that? I haven't thought about you in years." The words sting. "You were someone I knew once. But then you showed up on my door with a look in your eye I never thought you'd have." He takes a deep breath. "And now I can't stop thinking about you."

My mouth falls open as he wipes a stray hair from my face. "You're telling me everything I want to hear. But—"

"When you moved away, my life sucked." Rick opens his heart up to me, but all I can think about is Donovan.

How can he be saying this to me when I'm with someone else? And why do I care so much? I barely know Donovan, but that doesn't mean I want to hurt him.

"I was crushing on you bad, and you were my best friend," he went on. Then ..." Rick shrugs. "I had no one. But now you're back," he says, running his hands through my hair. "The Lara I loved as a kid has come back to me, so how can I stay away? How?"

He reaches into his pocket, pulls out a square plastic bag, and hands it to me. When I turn it over, I see a purple lollipop ring. Is it possible he's kept it all these years?

I glance up at him. "Oh, Rick ..."

He leans in and whispers with a quiet passion. "Why not leap at the chance? We'll solve this thing with your dad. Figure it out. Together." He clasps both his hands over mine, and I can't fight it anymore.

I close my eyes, and he kisses me. The kiss is perfect. It makes my heart sore, but something feels fake, wrong. His speech couldn't have been more what I wanted, but inside me something is breaking. When we pull away, our eyes meet, but despite everything I desire, I don't see that look in his eye. I don't see anything familiar.

"Are you sure—?"

"Is this what you mean by old friend?"

I gasp and spin around. Donovan is standing there with his hands in his pockets.

"It's not what you think. Don—"

"Not what I think?"

He's snarling and his hands are coiled. Behind him I see a posse of guys all using the same dress code of expensive jeans and finely pressed shirts. The natives are starting to circle, and I need to get Rick out of there before Donovan goes primeval.

Rick backs away, obviously sensing the danger, and I put my hand on Donovan's chest.

"It's not like that. We are old friends. Things got out of hand. Don, you have to believe me." I don't know why I care so stinking much, but the tears in my eyes say I do.

Donovan grunts. "Old friend, huh? Looks like it from his ripped jeans and nasty janitor's top. Late for work, Rick?"

Rick snorts and throws up his hands. "Whatever, man. You think you own her? You don't. Sorry your ego got bruised, but she can make her own choices. Call me when you're free of this guy, Lara."

He turns and walks away, but Donovan charges, punching him in the back. Rick sprawls to the ground onto his chest and slides along the floor. Donovan charges with his fists clenched, and I scream, grabbing at his arm to slow him down.

Behind me, the music stops. The twins are going to get off the carousel and see everyone fighting. It'll scare them, and Mom will never let me take them out again. Terrified, my mind spins. My feet dig into the tile as Donovan's friends laugh. I tug on his arm as hard as I can, grunting under the strain.

"Don, please. The kids are here."

He freezes at my words, and his face turns to stone. Rick gets up and shakes himself off. I try to apologize with my eyes, but his are ablaze with fury. I've seen it before, and things are going to get worse. The boys stare each other down.

"I think," I start carefully, "we should go our separate ways now."

I wrap my hand around Donovan's strong bicep, aware how wrong this is, but it relaxes his body. Kids around us are as waves in the ocean, bouncing and parting. I turn to find the twins when I hear a scream.

"Molly!"

Hearing Mike's cry sets my joints on fire. I charge against the mob of people, looking for my brother. I see him through the crowd running away from me, almost as if he's chasing after someone.

I push past everyone, hurrying to get to him. My arms pump, and I sprint as though I were in a race. Behind me, Donovan screams my name, but I keep going until I catch up to Mike. He's breathing hard and crying with his hands over his eyes.

Down on bended knee, I take him by the shoulders. "What's wrong? What happened?"

He points, unable to complete a sentence without babbling. Donovan joins us and gives Mike a light punch on the shoulder.

"We can't help you, dude, unless you tell us."

Mike takes a breath and composes himself. "Someone came on the carousel right as it stopped … He took Molly."

My heart stops, and my nose begins to bleed.

Chapter Thirteen

The mall goes into complete lockdown a few minutes too late. Whoever has taken Molly had enough time to get away. It's my fault. If I hadn't been fighting with Donovan and Rick, I would've seen it.

I should've been paying attention.

I sit on the edge of a carousel with a tissue pushed to my nose. The bleeding slows. The loud, angry crowd around us grows, increasingly irritated about being detained by the police. Kids cry, but none of them are Molly; she must be long gone. I can't help but wonder if my actions since being in this new past are to blame.

Donovan sits with Mike, who is crying hysterically, having rarely been separated from his twin, especially not in such a disturbing fashion. I worry he'll be traumatized forever if we don't get her back. I glance at my watch. It's only been fifteen minutes, but it feels as if it's been a lifetime. I wonder where Mom is and what I'll say to her, what she'll say to me. I wasn't supposed to take them out without permission.

And now Molly was gone. Like Mom hasn't been through enough. I remove the tissue and fold it up.

Rick sits beside me. "You all right?"

I nod but keep silent for fear of blubbering. I take a deep breath. "She's a baby, you know. Not even seven years old yet. I should've ... kept a better eye on her."

Rick swallows, and I see his neck muscles clenching. "I shouldn't have come." He shakes his head. "I didn't think kissing you would lead here."

"Me either," I whisper, barely able to get the words out.

I sit up straighter when I see Mike coming over. I hold my breath as he crushes me in a bear hug and buries his head deep in my stomach. I hold him as tight as I can, but my eyes are focused on Donovan, who is walking in front of me. I'm not sure I've ever seen a face more severe than Donovan's, his lips turned down and his eyes hollow.

He runs a hand through his hair as if he's getting ready to say something, but the charging of footsteps behind him distracts all of us. Mike looks up and cries, "Mom," and rushes toward our parents.

Mom and Jax are bent down low, ready to accept Mike's tackle of a hug, and my stomach twists. I don't want to live through what's coming. I'm not ready for the worry, the lecture. I pray they'll see how much this is killing me.

"I shouldn't have … started with Rick. If I knew the twins were here …" He chokes out the words, not on tears but instead on his pride.

I nod. "You didn't know." My tongue circles inside my mouth. I taste metal and something like fish. Is it nerves? Something else?

Glares of intimidation pass between Donovan and Rick. They have unfinished business, but it's going to have to wait.

Mom approaches me, her cheeks still streaked with tears and her green eyes lit like a Christmas tree. "What happened?" she demands.

Ready to face the music, despite the growing pit of dread in my stomach, my mouth opens.

"What the hell were you doing here?" she says before I can utter a word. "You said you had chores. You said you had homework. Why did you lie, Lara? Why!"

"We just—"

"She's a baby," Mom wobbles on her feet, and fresh tears spring to her eyes. "And now? Why can't you tell the truth once in a while? Why!" Her hands are shaking in the air, as if she wishes they were squeezing my neck.

I feel seething jealousy. She seems to love Molly more than me, so I take out the receipt from my purse, crumble it, and throw it at her. "Because they wanted to get you this. It was supposed to be a surprise. All right?"

Mom reads it, but her eyes barely flicker. I thought it might be my way of defusing the situation, but I lose hope as she tosses the receipt down on the floor. "Fine. A shopping trip? Fine. So where were you when she was taken? Why weren't you there the moment, the very moment, the ride stopped?"

Donovan steps forward. "It was my fault, Miranda. I'm sorry. I saw Lara with Rick. I … distracted her. I'm real sorry," he says with his eyes trained on me.

It means a lot that he'd take the blame after what he caught me doing. I bite my lip, waiting for Mom's next venomous attack. It's not really her fault, but it doesn't make it hurt less.

"Rick?" Her tone shows recognition. "I didn't know you still talked to him."

"It's a new thing," I say and grip my fingers.

Jax stands behind my mother, massaging her shoulders. I can't tell if he wants to kill me or not. "Police have some questions for Lara, if you agree."

Mom nods without thinking. "Anything. Anything that brings our baby home."

In two steps a police officer is beside me, and while his face is friendly, this feels like the beginning of the end.

****

The officers take me to a private room at the mall and ask me a lot of questions I don't have answers for, but I repeat to them what happened, making sure my story doesn't change. I even keep in the part about Donovan and Rick fighting because I'm sure someone has tipped them off. When they ask if I saw anything and I break down crying, they give me some tissues and a glass of water. Someone mentions reviewing the security tapes, which gives me an idea.

"Can't you go back in time? Follow who took her?"

The officers exchange glances. "We wish we could, but the red tape involved—"

"We would never get to her in time. Time travel is reserved for ... serial killers, and even then ..." The officer shakes his head, but it's obvious he wishes things were different.

So do I. Suddenly, everything Congress is voting on next week, what my mom has been working toward, doesn't seem so evil.

It seems necessary.

A knock comes from the door, and Jax pokes his head in. "It's been a long day for my son. Are you done with Lara?"

My heart feels run over with a cheese grater. The police dismiss me but say they'll be back in the morning with more questions. I don't know where we are going, but I put on my jacket, glad to be going somewhere other than here.

I wish I had never bought that stupid necklace. Even more, I wish I had never gone back in time. I miss my dad, my room, and my stupid mutt of a dog who forgot to go outside before he peed. I miss the Rick I knew and cold bowls of macaroni and cheese. God, how I miss Rick.

When we get into the elevator, I stare up at Jax. I've failed him, and I'm desperate for his approval. "I'm sorry."

I bite my lip and cover my eyes with both my hands to hide my tears, but my shoulders rock in heavy sobs. I'm not sure what I expect, but it isn't a warm embrace. I rest my head against his chest and everything in me lets go. He should be screaming at me, but all he does is rub my back and rest his chin on mine.

"You're my daughter too, you know. And I know no matter how bad things have been, I know how much you love Molly. I *know*."

My teeth chatter as I will myself to pull together. The elevator opens, and a police officer greets us and escorts us out the back of the mall, where cars are waiting to take us home. Jax opens the door and waits for me to slide beside Mom. I try not to look at her, and she's trying not to look at me. I don't know how bad it is, but I don't want to talk about it.

My parents talk about the police, and after a while Jax turns his attention to me, since Mom seems to be giving me the cold shoulder. "There will be police at the house to monitor our lines. They think we'll get a ransom call over the next day, and then we can get Molly back."

Sitting beside Jax, Mike's brown eyes are lost in an abyss of despair, and I wink at him to try to make him feel better. He gives me a sad smile, so I can tell he doesn't blame me, and I thank God for small favors.

We're all quiet the rest of the way home. It's getting dark, but as the car pulls up to the house I see the flash of cameras from the journalists camped out on our lawn. I close my eyes from dread as the door opens and a million questions are shouted at once.

An officer takes me by the arm and helps push me through the crowd. Mike cries through the rushing field of questions.

"Lara, this isn't the first time tragedy has struck your family. Why do you think that is?"

"Lara, when you noticed your sister was missing, how did this make you feel?"

Lara. Lara. Lara.

The door to the house is flung open by an FBI agent, and I quickly duck in. Mom's face is severe as she carries Mike through the door. When Jax slams the door shut I jump, and feeling the start of a headache coming on, I rub my temples.

Not now. I don't want any new memories now. The ones I have are enough to kill me.

Through the glass, the lights continue to flicker, and I turn from them to watch Mom carrying Mike up the stairs. It'll be a long night for him, for all of us.

Jax rests his hand on my shoulder and squeezes me close as he listens to the FBI agents. I miss what they say as the pounding in my head grows louder. I feel as if I'm in a tunnel underwater, and nothing around me seems real.

It's like a bad dream, and I'm desperate to wake up. My head flashes.

****

I see twin babies in front of me. Each of them is in a walker, one blue and the other pink, but neither baby is big enough to move their walker, thanks to the deep, plush carpet.

I sit on the floor with them, legs crossed. I cover my eyes, wiggle my fingers, and yell, "Boo!"

They giggle with excitement, and I kiss each of their chubby hands.

Laughter comes from behind me. Jax is sitting on the sofa with his paperwork spread out in front of him. With glee in my head, I bounce on the sofa and fold myself against him. He squeezes me as hard as he can and plants kisses on my forehead.

"You love the twins?"

"They're the best." I grin and peer up at him. He kisses my nose. "When's Mom coming home?"

"Soon." Jax nods. "A rough few weeks at work but she'll be here soon. She misses you guys something fierce when she has to work late like this, you know that?"

"Yeah," I say, but a darkness in my heart begins to swallow me. Jax always says that, but when she is home, all she does is take care of the twins.

"Maybe Mom can take me to see a movie sometime?" I ask with hope, my knees knocking together. "Just the two of us?"

"Now there's an idea. I bet she'd love it." He winks at me, and we settle in for a few minutes and watch TV.

When the front door slams, I get excited and stand up to greet Mom. She's rushing in with a giant smile on her face.

"Hi sweetheart," she says to me, but her eyes dart quickly to the twins. She squeals and begins to scoop them up.

My heart falls, and I sink back into the sofa cushions, feeling invisible. I wish they'd swallow me alive. Maybe then Mom would notice me.

****

The intense pain in my head is gone as the memory fades, but now I'm forced to live with the truth that I've felt left out in my family for a long time. I am essentially the third wheel in the Montgomery home and a painful reminder of John Crane.

Lara was right. The Lara I became that is.

Me, I was wrong.

"When do you think the call will come in?" Jax says, and my head snaps to attention.

"Soon. By tomorrow night."

Jax runs a hand through his hair. "Tomorrow *night*? She's only a little girl." He bites his lip, and I'm sorry for hating him a few days ago. I see the fear in his eyes and know how much he loves Molly.

I try to move away, but his arm is clamped hard around me. He doesn't seem to want me to escape, so I stand there and stare at the floor.

Clomping footsteps come down the stairs. "Go to your room," Mom orders me. She stands at the bar and pours herself a stiff drink. She downs it without looking at me and commands, "Go."

"Miranda." Jax's eyes narrow. "She has every right to be—"

"Don't argue with me tonight. Not tonight." She clenches her jaw, refusing to look at either of us.

Jax hugs me, and I bury my face against his neck. "It'll be easier tomorrow," he whispers against my ear. "I love you, peanut."

I flood with love for him along with regret. I want to hug Mom, tell her I'm sorry, but she doesn't want to hear it.

I rush past her with my head ducked down and take the stairs two at a time. Once I'm in my room, I slam the door, plop myself on the bed, and cry until every tear in me is drained. I fall asleep with my mouth propped open, and drool runs down onto my pillow.

****

It's eight in the morning, but I don't remember dreaming or the passage of time. Suddenly, my eyes are open, my chest is tight with anxiety, and the memories of losing Molly at the mall crash into me like a freight truck.

No one has woken me, and there isn't any noise from downstairs. I'm guessing today I won't be going to school, but I don't want to go downstairs and hang out with my mom all day. I have things I need to figure out. I still need answers, and I can't find them being stuck inside the house all day.

I get up and put on a pair of jeans and the darkest navy hoodie I can find, navy, which is better than nothing. I brush out my long hair and tie my curls back in a ponytail. I check the mirror. My face looks exhausted, and my eyes are haunted.

I hear a knock at my door. I hold my breath and close my eyes, waiting for whoever it is to go away. When I think they've gone away, the knocks renew.

"Lara, you awake?" Jax's voice is full of sadness and worry, and I don't have any choice. I go over and pull open the door.

Jax is standing with a small tray full of breakfast goodies, wearing a t-shirt and jeans, which I haven't seen him in before. From the worn expression on his face, I don't think he slept at all last night.

"Thought you might be hungry."

"Thanks," I say, doing my best to smile as I take the tray from him and put it down on my desk. My stomach rumbles as I look at the muffins and Danish. I wish he had put a cup of coffee on there, but it'll do. "Any word?" I ask, unable to look at him.

"Not yet, but the FBI thinks the call will come tonight. We need to stay here and … wait."

Trying not to cry again, I say, "Good to know."

"You can come downstairs. Mike needs the distraction. Mom … she's calmer. She'd like to talk to you."

"That's why you came to bring me breakfast, right?" I ask bitterly.

Jax places a hand on my shoulder. "Come down when you can."

I sit down and bite into a muffin. It tastes good, but I can't enjoy it. Not really. If I never see Molly again, I'm not sure how I'll ever enjoy anything again.

After breakfast, I get ready, but I take my time. I'm in no rush to head downstairs or to the confrontation that's sure to follow. I jump when my phone rings and hunt it down in my purse.

"Hello?" I say, even though I don't recognize the number.

"You have two days." I can't tell if the digitized voice is a man or a woman.

"Two days for what?" I ask, feeling my gut tighten.

"Two days to return what belongs to me, Ms. Montgomery, or you will never see your sister again."

I glance over my shoulder at the door, and the voice continues, "Don't go to your parents or the police. If you do, I'll see that Molly dies, and it will not be easy for her. Understood?"

Is he watching me? I go to my window and lift my blinds. "How do I get it back to you?"

"We will call you again tomorrow morning. Make sure you don't miss the call."

The line goes dead.

Every nerve in my body tingles, feels on fire. I have no idea what he's talking about, or where I might be hiding it, but I need to find out.

Fast.

Molly's life depends on it.

Chapter Fourteen

I take another bite of my breakfast and chug some milk before I collect my things. I hurry down the stairs, slinging my book bag over my shoulder as I reach the living room. A few FBI agents are sitting on the sofa, and the coffee table has been converted to a workstation with computers, monitors, and equipment I don't recognize.

Mike crushes me in a full body assault hug as soon as I enter the room, bringing me to my knees. "I'm sorry, Lara. I'm sorry." His eyes are glistening.

I stroke his hair back, feeling like road kill because he feels the need to apologize. "I'm the one that should be apologizing to you. It's not your fault. It's mine. All mine."

"You told me to keep an eye on her, but I didn't. I was excited and forgot." Mike hangs his head and bites his lip.

The disappointment on his face burns my heart. "Did I say anything else? When I told you to take care of Molly, what else did I say?"

He shrugs and gets a far off look on his face. "Dunno. Only … keep her close. And to look out—"

"Look out?" I edge him on with quiet urgency. "Look out for … ?"

"The woman with the purple hair."

A scene flashes in my mind. Something cold like metal presses against my neck, and then electricity is jolting through my body. The world goes dark as I'm thrown into the back of a van.

When I can see again, a dark, shaded face, framed by purple hair, leans in and whispers to me. "You have to protect that video you took at all costs. If anyone finds out you have it, they'll kill you."

I flash back to the present with no idea when or where this happened. Did this happen to me? Or the other Lara before I changed the past?

I leave Mike to go to the bathroom. I flip the light on and peer at my neck, where I felt the jolt of electricity, and sure enough I see two purple marks on my neck. As if I was attacked by a vampire.

Or a taser.

I take my hair out of its ponytail and ruffle it along my shoulders, so no one else will see. When I exit again, Mike is gone and Mom is standing there waiting for me. Her eyes are rimmed red. If there is a hell, she appears to be there.

"Hi," I say quietly, awkwardly. I don't know what else I'm supposed to say.

She frowns and comes to me. Putting her hands on my shoulders, she kisses my head and pulls me in for a deep, warm hug. I close my eyes and give a relieved sigh. I lie against her, wishing she could hold me forever.

"I never should've—last night—I'm so sorry, Lara. You're hurting. I'm hurting. I shouldn't have."

I nod but can't speak.

"You're my baby too. You know that? But Molly is only a little girl. I … get so scared. I don't want to lose any of my babies, ever."

"We've been through a lot lately."

She strokes my hair from my face and kisses my forehead, her chin quivering. "That we have."

"I guess we really need that vacation once Molly gets back."

"Umm-hmm, once she gets back," Mom whispers. "We'll have the best time. She loves it when you take her down the water slides."

"Me too. Can't wait to do it again. I promised her …" My voice trails off as I'm hit with a memory.

I sit on Molly's bed. Around her neck is a locket, inside which I attach a tiny computer chip. She smiles at me.

"Keep it safe for me, Moll."

She nods, happy and relaxed. She thinks it's a game.

But it's not.

What if that was what the man on the phone wanted? What if Molly has it? Would I be stupid enough to steal something from someone dangerous and hide it on my baby sister?

I'm pretty sure the answer is an obvious yes. Making good decisions is not my best trait, I think it's fair to say. "Ahem … Mom, do you mind if I go out? I need to do some research for a paper I'm doing. Plus, it's a team report. I need to get Donovan to help me."

Mom shakes her head adamantly. "Absolutely, not."

"Mom—"

"I said no, Lara. Your school will understand. I'm never letting another one of my girls out of my sight again."

I relent as I begin coming up with a plan. "Okay, I'll be up in my room. Need to do a few things."

I bump into Jax in the hall. "Things better now with your Mom?"

"Yeah. Things are as good as they're going to get until …" My voice trails off as I stare at the carpet.

Jax sighs. "Please try not to upset your Mom anymore. She's been through enough."

"I won't. Promise." I hug him and he squeezes me real tight, until I can barely breathe. "We'll see Molly soon, I know it."

He chokes on a sob, trying hard to maintain control.

I kiss his cheek. "I love you, Dad."

The words escape my lips even before I realize I'm saying them. I feel shock flood my face. How can I feel that Jax is my dad? My dad is in prison. How does any of this make sense? I can only think of one reason; I'm losing the Lara I was and melding into the new one.

Jax pats my cheek. "Been so long since I've heard that. I'm real glad, Lara. Real glad."

"Me too."

I barely eke out the words before ducking into my bedroom. I grab my backpack and stuff it with everything I think I'll need before I toss it out my bedroom window. I turn on some music, so they'll think I'm studying or something. Hopefully, no one will realize I've snuck out for at least an hour. After making sure the coast is clear, I sneak out my window and start the trek to Donovan's house, careful to stay off the main roads, where police might find me.

The door is answered by a servant, who ushers me into the grand entryway. The floors are marble, and lush curtains frame the dozen elegant windows.

"I will let Donovan know you are here, Miss." He leaves with a bow.

I peek into the family sitting room. It's equally as breathtaking and elegant. Family portraits stare down from the wall above the brick fireplace. I go inside and touch the leather sofa—soft as a baby's bum. On the glass tabletop beside the sofa is a lamp and a plaque. I pick up the plaque. *Rewind's MVP Two Years running.*

This is why I'm here. I need answers only Senator Patricia James would've, but if Donovan feels as protective about his parents as I do of mine, I need to be extremely careful.

As I consider my plan of attack, an unstoppable memory dances on the edge of my mind.

****

I am young, maybe five, and sitting in the apartment I shared with my parents before Mom died. It's a large brownstone, not great but nicer than where I would grow up after she died. I'm playing with an assortment of blocks when an argument from the kitchen draws my attention.

"It's only dinner, John. A work dinner. You know how important my research—"

"Another one? Every week it's another excuse to work late, Miranda. I can't keep leaving work early to pick up Lara from daycare. I'm going to lose my job."

During a moment of silence I sneak over to the kitchen. I hear Mom mumbling, but I can't make out the words.

"Oh, don't give me that!" Dad rages, throwing his hands over his head in frustration.

"My job is important. I'm onto something big, John, big. If I can do it, I will get a promotion, maybe be in charge of the whole department one day. Do you know what that means for you? For Lara?" Mom pours pasta from a pot into a strainer for my evening dinner of mac and cheese.

"Don't pretend it's about us. It hasn't been about *us* in a long time. You're getting too ambitious. What about us having another baby?"

"I want that. Of course I do. I love you, John. More than anything. Please don't make this about something it's not. One dinner this week. One. That's all I'm asking. Please."

Dad finally agrees, nodding. They embrace long and warm, making me smile.

"And this Mr. Montgomery, he isn't good looking, is he?" Dad jokes.

Mom laughs. "Not as handsome as you. No one could make me want to give you up, don't you know that?"

"When you look at me like that I do."

****

Mom was having dinner with Jax.

This news hits me like a ton of bricks. Maybe they were only colleagues who became closer during the trial. Or maybe what I don't want to admit is true. Mom was having an affair, and Dad was suspicious, but she was ready to cut it off based on her resignation letter. She loved Dad and didn't want to give up on him. When someone tried to kill her, she obviously changed her mind, at least when Dad became the lead suspect.

"Hey," Donovan says, snapping me from my thoughts.

I leap up. "Hi. Can we talk?"

He nods and leads me up the stairs. His large room is decorated in simple browns and tans. I sit on the edge of his giant bed, and he sits beside me, but for a long while we are an ocean's breadth away until his hand slowly inches out to mine. When his fingers squeeze mine, I squeeze back. I look in his eyes and see his sadness, his regret. I feel it too.

"I shouldn't have kissed Rick," I say, the truth of the words crushing my chest like a boulder. "I'm sorry."

"Why'd you do it?" His words echo around us as if we're in a grand hall.

"It was a dream, the childish dream of a girl who moved away when she was eight." I twist my lip to the side. "Then the dream was in front of me, and it just happened."

Donovan stares at me, unblinking. "Just happened." His voice is void of emotion.

"I know that doesn't make it easier."

"Makes it worse." His words lash out at me.

"Will we be okay?" I asked.

"I don't know," he says, turning towards me.

I fall silent, wishing I could take the kiss back. I wish Donovan hadn't seen it.

"No word yet?" he asks.

Grateful for the change in topic, I shake my head. "Not yet. They think they'll call by tonight."

His eyes widen. "Man. She's so ... little."

"Do you remember when your Mom worked at Rewind?"

He gives me a funny look. "That's a strange question."

"Humor me."

His eyebrows rise. "Well, not much. I was pretty young. I remember seeing you there." He knocks his knee into mine.

I laugh nervously. The touch of his skin against mine makes me shiver. My heart leaps, but I wish it hadn't. I don't know what's happening, but I'm beginning to feel more comfortable with Donovan than with Rick. I smile, and my hand edges further into his. He clasps his other hand over mine tightly. I can remember loving Rick, kissing Rick, but I can't remember what it felt like.

Donovan leans in to kiss me, and I hesitate. I think of Rick, everything we shared in the past, everything already gone because I traded it in for this crazy world. Could I win it back? My feelings for Donovan were growing. Could I risk what I feel for Donovan, everything we've built, for the hope Rick might really fall in love with me one day?

I bite my lip, and Donovan strokes my cheek with the back of his hand. "What are you so afraid of?" His eyes are sincere, warm.

"That I love you. That I might lose you too. That I'm a screw up caught in the middle of this big thing I can't talk about."

"We'll figure it out together," he whispers.

When he moves to kiss me, I have no will left to resist. I close my eyes and lean forward to meet his lips. I welcome his urgent kisses. I welcome the distraction. Simply feeling that someone wants me, that he loves and appreciates me, feels good. Rick will never love me as he used to. I can tell that from the look in his eye, and when I'm with Donovan, love and warmth fills me. I'm afraid to think about what that means.

Donovan kisses me harder, more passionately. His arms tighten around me, and I wish the world would fade away. I wish I could forget about saving my dad, Molly, everyone and stay there.

"Thank you," I whisper for a million reasons, and a shocked smile spreads over Donovan's face. "For not giving up on me."

"I can't imagine how hard things were for you last night." I see the worry, the fear in his eyes.

I nod. "I need to tell you something, but you can't tell anyone else." When he promises he won't, I continue. "The kidnappers called me. They want something of theirs I have."

His eyes bug. "You have to tell the police."

"I can't," I insist. "They'll hurt Molly."

He takes a deep breath and gazes off into the distance, clearly thinking. "Then we'll have to go get the papers."

My heart jumps. "You know what they're talking about?"

He stares at me, incredulous. "Is now the time for jokes? Of course I know where they are. You hid them at the YMCA."

Suddenly everything is crystal clear. The key in my wallet is a locker key. My mouth falls open in shock. I try to cover it up but no such luck.

"You really didn't remember?"

"It's been a hard week, okay?" I shrug him off, defensive.

"Okay, okay," he says, holding his hands up.

I try to hide my smirk. "Sorry. So this is all I need? Just the key. Well, that seems pretty easy—"

Donovan shakes his head. He takes me by the arm and leads me out of his room into a home office. He goes under the desk, where I hear him pull something from underneath. He reaches out and pops a flash drive into my hand.

The flash drive.

"This is it," I whisper to myself, but Donovan thinks I'm talking to him.

"Part of it. You get the paper documents. Then you have everything." He smooths my hair and kisses my lips. "Be careful."

I nod, hanging onto him. "This isn't good-bye."

His eyes twinkle. "It better not be."

We walk to the front door, and I pause on the front steps. "Donovan, be careful."

He nods.

I turn the corner around some bushes, finally on the street, and two police officers step out from their squad car. I swear under my breath as I nearly crash into them.

"Ms. Montgomery, your parents are looking for you."

If getting into trouble was a career, I'd be at the top of the ladder.

Chapter Fifteen

Hiding out in my room might be a bad idea, but that's exactly what I do. Mom comes in and sits on my bed but is silent for too long, making me anxious.

"Lara," she laments, "you know how worried we were?"

"You're not going to yell at me?" I ask. "I'd yell at me."

"Then why do it? Why sneak out and go to Donovan's?"

A lot of answers would work, but I decide to go with the truth. "I was tired of being alone and scared. He ... always makes me feel better."

She exhales. "It's me. I drove you to him by how I acted last night. God, I'm sorry, Lara." She strokes my hair off my face. "I'm real sorry. I didn't mean to make you feel any of those things."

"Yes you did," I whisper.

Shock fills her face, but she nods and tears glisten in her eyes. "You're right, and that makes me even sadder and angrier at myself."

We hold hands. "I'm glad you're not mad."

She gives a short burst of nervous laughter. "Well, how can I be? My daughter has been kidnapped. I'm glad you're okay."

"Can I ask you something?"

She nods. "Of course."

"When did you fall in love with Jax?"

Her mouth falls in astonishment. "Lara, where is this coming from?"

"Please tell me. Honestly. Please."

She rubs her hands on her pants and shifts. "The moment I met him, the attraction was instant, and I did my best to avoid him, keep it at bay, but we spent a lot of time together. And your father … I loved him too, but we were under a lot of stress. We lost our way."

"When did Dad find out?"

She shrugs and tucks her hair behind her ears. "I didn't think he knew. After the day in the alley, I swore I'd never see Jax again. I'd move us to the mountains in a log cabin if I had to." She laughs bitterly.

"So you wanted to stay?"

"Of course I did! But after the police started questioning your Dad, he changed. He became jumpy, and then … our life changed forever." I watch her twist her wedding ring around her finger. "We waited until after the trial to date again and got married a year later. We were happy … and I never expected to get pregnant again." She takes a deep breath. "But it's been a good life. We've been happy, for the most part."

"I'm sorry I'm such a crummy daughter," I say, wringing my hands together.

"You're doing what you're supposed to be doing. I'm the one who needs to step it up." She kisses my cheeks.

"Does Rewind have you working on stuff that's illegal?"

Her eyes cloud over. "Where is this coming from?"

"I saw it … in the paper. Some reporter's questions."

"Memory storage isn't illegal!" she says, standing up. "It's a good company and not one to mess around with illegal things. Don't listen to those phony articles; they are designed to sell magazines. Don't worry, Lara. My job is perfectly safe. Once we get Molly back, everything will go back to normal."

Her tone signals the conversation is over. Even though I know she's lying, part of me believes her. She's as good a liar as I am.

Once she leaves, I make my plan to escape. I need to head to the YMCA and find those papers, but I look out the window and see two police officers guarding the premises. There's no way I can get out while it's still light. Hopefully, I can get out later, when it's dark and people are beginning to fall asleep.

That's my plan.

I only have thirty hours left.

***

I pack a duffle bag for the night. As I'm storing a flashlight, I hear a rumbling downstairs about an early dinner. Everyone is on edge, so I go out quietly, but I bump into Jax in the hall by the front steps. His eyes flash with surprise, and then I see sadness, anger cross his face.

"Dad," I say softly, reaching for his arm, "I'm sorry about this morning, sneaking out after we talked."

He nods, and for a brief moment I'm off the hook. "You always promise, and you never mean it, Lara. That's the problem. You're ... too spontaneous. You need to think sometimes about how your actions affect other people." He turns and leaves for the stairs, leaving me feeling guilty.

But I can get her back. I just need some time away from the FBI.

I head downstairs to eat pizza with the family. We have a quiet, strange dinner in the living room, while the agents eat against the wall. The entire thing is like a weird sort of funeral or wake, where no one wants to talk, but a deep foreboding fog hangs over the room. I can think of no chit chat that would be worthy of the space, and apparently neither can anyone else. Even Mike folds his pizza three times before being content enough to bite into it.

I need to get some medicine soon to cut off the edge of an oncoming headache before I have a full blown incident. I stand up and am mentioning getting a drink from the kitchen when I hear a crash upstairs.

Everyone jumps to their feet, and Jax pulls Mike in close to his chest to protect him. Two agents sprint up the stairs while two stay with us. Everyone thinks someone is inside the house, but I'm safe and at ease as if everything will be okay.

"Lara," Mom says painfully.

My eyes flash to the anchor talking on the TV. I grab the remote to raise the volume. "It seems, Jack, that the guards were able to gather control in the prison shortly after the riot broke out. There were a few injuries, but only one inmate was critically injured, and he's being rushed to MGH Hospital via helicopter. His name hasn't yet been released to the hospital, but next of kin will be notified."

That's the prison Dad is in. When the phone rings behind Mom, I know what the news will be.

But Jack the anchor isn't done yet. He continues. "What about leaked reports that a woman was seen inside the prison with ... purple hair?"

Everything in me grows still, and I turn to Mom, who is holding the receiver in mid-air. There's something I haven't seen on her face before.

Fear.

"You know her?" I demand, walking up to her. "You know the woman with the purple hair?"

She shakes her head. "No, I … I don't know who she is …"

"Liar," I snarl. "It's written all over your face. Who is she?"

She hangs up the phone. "I don't know! Well, I have seen her. Flashes. Like a ghost. B-b-but-but I have no idea who she is." She cries into her hands.

"Does she work with you? The senator?"

"What do you know about my work with the senator?" Her nostrils flare.

The FBI agents are back behind us, apparently unable to find anyone in the house, which should make me feel better, but it doesn't. Jax and Mike are still there, but I've forgotten them as I stare down my mother.

"Enough," I spit out. "Enough to know you're into illegal research. That memory storage is nothing but a cover."

Mom gasps. "You went through my papers? In my office? Damn it, Lara! Do you have any idea what you've done!"

My chest puffs up. "Well, excuse me if I needed information. I needed answers, and you never give me anything. Everything is all hugs and kisses, and oh, we'll go on vacation soon, but you know what? Vacation never comes. You've been saying this for years. Years! So what's so damn important that you can't talk to me? Spend time with us? We were supposed to be a family!"

Mom cries into her fist, but I don't care.

"Why is working for the senator so important that you'd throw us all away!"

Jax tugs on my shoulders. "Enough, Lara! Your mom has been through enough. Up to your room."

I spin on my heels, wanting to wave my finger in his face. He doesn't know what I've done, what I've given up.

"Now, young lady," Jax scolds me with brow furrowed, peering down at me over his nose. He's never looked at me like that. Ever.

I need to do what he says, and I have never felt so alone.

Up in my room, I swallow my pain medicine, take a few sips of water, and set my alarm. Angry as I am, all I can think about is my plan to save Molly.

I wake up in the dark with my head throbbing and waves of pain colliding into me. The red glow from the clock blinking *8:00 PM* is all I can see. The ticking of my heart in my brain is louder than it should be.

I groan, fall to my knees beside the bed, and squeeze the bridge of my nose. This is it. Whatever time travel sickness is, it's going to claim me. I feel as if someone is taking a vegetable peeler up and down my bones, exposing muscle, and then pouring salt over my open wounds.

I manage to crawl over to the desk and snap on my desk lamp after several tries. My limbs don't want to listen to the commands I give them. I reach up, find my bottle of ibuprofen, and fumble with the lid.

The pressure in my head builds as tablets spill everywhere. I scoop some up and swallow them dry. I'm not even sure how many, but I'm in misery, and I might go insane if this agony doesn't stop. I rest my head on the desk as tears dribble down my cheeks. I hear banging at my door and realize I've been screaming.

"Lara?" Jax bangs again.

"Daddy?"

Briefly, a vision dances just out of my sight. It ebbs and flows out of my reach like a skipping record on a DJ's turntable. My fingers grip the carpet, and as the pounding in my brain gets worse, I eke out a scream and fold forward, cowering, tearing at the fibers. I never thought pain could be this intense. My body fights the vision, part of me desperate to hold back the oncoming memory. My door is kicked open, and the crack of the wood slamming into the wall makes my brain burn.

"Oh my God, Lara!" Jax takes me by the shoulders and pulls me back onto his chest. I quake in a spasm, his touch alone enough to drive me to shrieks. "Miranda!" he screams, unaware how badly he's hurting me.

I glance up at him and mumble, "I'm sorry."

Those are surely my last words. His face spins, but as the world begins to dim, my brain clicks like a puzzle.

Mom screams and clutches at my legs. "Baby? Lara! How many pills did you take?"

As my consciousness begins to slip away, I can only stare up at Jax's face. It's older than I remember. Before, his hair was black and his eyes brown instead of blue.

But I am certain, one hundred percent certain.

He's the shooter from the alley.

Chapter Sixteen

Mom and Jax stay with me while the ambulance comes. While I am aware of them touching me, begging me to hold on, my mind isn't there.

It's elsewhere, gone.

In the past.

****

I hurry determinedly down the hall of an office building between two rows of cubicles, as though I belong there and know exactly where I'm going. I am dressed in blue heels, skinny jeans, and a dark blazer. A visitor's pass flaps from my lapel, and over my shoulder I carry my backpack. Telephones around me buzz, and people are leaned back, wearing headsets and taking calls. Must be a sales area.

I come to an office door. The brass plate in the center says *Jax Montgomery*. Glancing over my shoulder, I bite my lip before giving a pretend knock and slipping inside. His office has a glorious view of the Boston skyline. I quickly draw the shades, take off my backpack, and hurry over to his desk, which is covered in photos of our family and me. Seeing them, I burn with a red hot rage, but I push it down, so I can go through his desk drawers.

I don't find what I'm searching for there, but I do manage to gain access to his computer with his password and find one of the documents I need. While it prints, I run to the filing cabinet and search those drawers one at a time. Coming up empty, I move to the larger cabinet against the wall and find a manila folder under a stack of papers.

Bending down, I balance it on my knee as I flip through the records—Names, dates, everything I need. I also find black and white photos of Dad—my real dad, John Crane—taken with a long lens. They are surveillance photos, ones of my mom on her daily walk to work, the day some unknown person saved her, and my life changed forever. The day I lost my dad.

I'll do anything to get him back.

Anything.

I have to try.

Running back to the computer, I stick in my flash drive. Rewind must be stopped. I copy over every file I can find about their mind-scrubbing technology. Although new, they will perfect it with time. They will use it on people.

I can't let that happen. Jax, my Mom, the senator, I am going to bring them all down. What first started as an investigation about my dad has now turned into a crusade. It's bigger than me and my dad. It's about a million people's lives and what will happen if the senator keeps her power.

But I've connected the dots. The senator is responsible for trying to have my mom killed because she wanted to leave Rewind. And when that failed, she framed my dad. Afterwards, Mom changed her mind about leaving Rewind and fell deeper into research, trying to bury the pain of what John Crane did to her. And through it all, the responsible party wooed and married her and became my stepfather.

They all deserve to burn in hell.

The doorknob turns, and I pull my flash drive free. I won't be safe with the data until I get it to Joyce Meyers, so she can bring it to the press. I run to the printer and shove the papers into my backpack. As Jax steps into the room, I finish zipping it up and sling it over my shoulder. Steadying my breath, I brush my perfectly straight hair out of my face.

"Hi Daddy," I say and grin from ear to ear.

Jax masks his surprise with a smile and comes over to kiss my cheek. I do my best not to grit my teeth or clench my jaw. He always notices stuff like that. "Well, I didn't know you were coming today. We have a lunch date I forgot about?"

I shake my head. "Nothing official. Only here to apply for the internship next year." I hold up the badge I'm wearing around my neck.

His face lights up with pride, and he sits on the edge of his desk. "We'd be lucky to have you here. You are a chip off the old block."

I smile and nod, something I'm good at these days.

"Why don't I take you to lunch anyway? We don't get to do it enough anymore."

He puts his hand on my shoulder and gives me a squeeze. I remember when I loved it. I remember when I loved him, but all I feel now is betrayal, and when I tried to talk to Mom, she blew me off as though I were a liar, a freak. All I want is to know the truth. My dad—the man I only remember in flashes—deserves to know too.

"I'd love it," I say, and we link hands as we leave his office. I watch him in my periphery, but my eye is trained on the prize.

It's almost time to put my plan into motion.

****

Consciousness slams back into my body. With my eyes closed, I hear the soft hum of machines and sense the presence of people around me. I try to process what happened, what I know.

The Lara I was pieced together the details of Mom's attempted murder and knew she could find a trail back to her stepfather. All those memories of Jax loving me and tucking me into bed cut me like a knife.

But why?

Why do that to us? Why marry the woman he wanted dead and then keep her alive all these years? Why have children with her? Why be so kind to me? Was he too working for Senator Patricia James and keeping an eye on my mother, so she wouldn't step out of line?

Did he ever really love me?

It can't matter. My real dad has spent the last ten years of his life in prison, and I have to get him out. I have to finish what Lara started even if it means pissing off my mom, who let's face it, is pretty mad at me to begin with.

The first step is for me to get out of here somehow and get to Lara's stash, so I can piece together her plan and whether she let anyone in on her secret. More than once Donovan has referenced *the plan*, but I thought it was a shallow reference to the prom. What if I was wrong? What if I was wrong about everything?

I try to raise my eyelids, which feel weighted with stones. At first, my vision is blurry, as if I'm peering up from beneath water. My parents are talking at the foot of my bed. Out the window beyond them I see what appears to be the dawn sky with a trace of morning in the clouds.

How long was I out, and how has my injury inconvenienced Molly's kidnappers? If there was a kidnapper at all. Given the circumstances, I have no choice but to suspect Jax was involved.

My hand creeps up my face to the oxygen tubes inside my nostrils. How far has my health deteriorated? I must have given my mom quite a scare. I only hope I have enough time.

"Mom?" I finally croak out, sounding like an old man.

Her head jerks towards me, and she rushes to sit beside me. In one hand, she has a death grip on a tissue, and with the other she strokes my hair.

"Lara, baby?" I don't think she can say anything else as her body appears rocked with emotion. When she leans down to hug me, I cherish it.

"I'll get the doctor." Jax says and steps out into the hall.

I grip Mom's arms as she hugs me, burying her face in my hair. This is the closest I've felt to her since I changed the past. Part of me cherishes it, and another part wants to keep my distance because I don't know how long it's going to last.

"I'm sorry." I edge the words out of my mouth like a reluctant jumper. "About Molly. About—"

She shakes her head, eyes squeezed shut. "You didn't know. It wasn't your fault. I shouldn't have ... I shouldn't have made you feel like it was your fault." Her voice quivers, and the tears in her voice make it almost impossible to understand her. "I'm the one who is never around. It's my fault. Mine."

"No, Mom—" I shake my head, wanting to tell her everything that's wrong—why Jax is married to her.

"To think, you took all those pills because of me, of how I treated you." She blinks and laughs bitterly, such as when your emotions are so strong, you have no options left. "You've said before how I make you feel, but I never knew ... how true it was."

"Mom." I gain strength as she takes a deep breath. "I wasn't trying to kill myself. I only wanted to stop the pain. My head …"

She nods quickly, seeming to know the answer I'm about to give, but the lines on her face tell me she doesn't believe me. She really thinks I was going to kill myself. All these years with me and she doesn't know Lara Montgomery at all. But my dad, John Crane, he'd know I never give up. No matter what.

The door opens, and a doctor comes in with Jax. Mom stands and shakes his free hand. In the other he carries an X-ray. He smiles at me, the type of smile you never want to see. Forced, required. One you give someone sick, not someone about to get better. But at least my head is no longer splitting in two, giving me hope that all this might be coming to an end. Which, considering I have a baby sister to rescue, a father to free, and a stepfather I need to prove murdered my mother in another time line, is a good thing.

I tune out their conversation. The doctor slides my CT scans against a backlit frame, and I watch the picture of my brain glow to life. Something about it stills the room. Even though I have no idea what I'm looking at, my heart is in my throat, preventing me from swallowing. I can barely even breathe.

Mom's eyes twitch, and her hand covers her mouth. "That's not possible," she mutters to herself.

"Impossible as it is, I wish I could give you better news. I'm sorry, Ms. Montgomery." The doctor's eyes are on me, and the sadness in them says my diagnosis isn't good, that I don't have much time left. But I don't believe him. I can't.

"The bleeding in your brain is severe. I'm not sure if I can stop it. A neurosurgeon is on his way. He'll see you as soon as he gets here."

I go numb. Even my fingers won't work right. I nod my head and glance at my grief-stricken mother before my eyes fall to Jax. His face is crestfallen and his eyes moist. I can't help but wonder why he worries so much whether I live or die. I'm not his, and all of this is his fault anyway, so why care so damn much?

"The IV drip should keep you comfortable until the specialist arrives." He pauses, but no one moves to speak. Does he expect us to thank him?

I shouldn't be surprised at my brain injury. I signed up for it the moment I jumped into the past. I have no one to blame but myself, but I'm still angry I didn't get the fairytale I wanted.

The silence is interrupted as the door shuts behind the doctor. No one moves or speaks. Jax grips my foot. His eyes are intense as they lock with mine, and his chin trembles as he strives to regain control.

"I would like some time alone with Lara," Mom says with a hushed voice, as though speaking over a grave. Her face has gone cold as ice, practically unreadable. "Head home, in case the kidnapper calls."

Jax blinks, surprise lighting up his face like a freeway sign. "I can't leave."

Mom folds a corner of my blanket repeatedly, her head ducked too far down for me to read her expression. "Think of Molly. We can't abandon her. Please, Jax."

The silence multiplies the space between us until I feel stranded in the middle of a desert. Jax walks over. I try my hardest not to look at him, but I finally let him grip my hand as I turn my head. I am perplexed by his concern for me. He pivots and leaves without a final word. It's better that way I tell myself, but it still stings.

Mom stands up and goes to the wall, staring at my brain scan. I hold my breath as her finger traces over the gaps between my hemispheres, signifying small pools of blood.

"I've seen this before." Her voice is high, unnatural, barely holding her emotion together. "I've seen this a million times, so why don't you tell me what you've done."

Licking my lips, I consider how I should play it. "I'm not sure what you mean." Denial still seems my best alternative.

She spins to me. Her face is harried, as if she's spent all night pacing in the wings. It's possible she has. She's at my bedside in a moment's breath and gripping the sheet around my body.

"I work with time travel for a living, Lara. I've seen the case studies for those that tried to change their past." Her arm reaches straight out to point at the wall. "And that is it. I've watched them suffer, and then I've watched them die. So why don't you tell me ..." Her eyes are a blaze of anger, but her lips scrunch, "... if it was worth it."

My eyes fall away to the bed, and I shake my head as she sits beside me and takes me by the shoulders. "I didn't—"

"You hate our life with Jax so much you've invented this story. You think of your father as an innocent cub, but was it really worth your life being over?"

I remain silent, and she shakes me.

"Lara Montgomery! Answer me!"

I look up at her, and rage builds in my chest so intense I think I might choke on it. I grit my teeth and whisper, "My name's Lara Crane, and I'm not who you think I am."

Chapter Seventeen

The color drains from Mom's face, and she sits on the seat beside my bed. It makes sense she would assume I'm her Lara, out to prove to everyone John Crane was innocent of murder. Now I know a very important fact: Lara told Mom about her suspicions that Jax framed John Crane.

But did Mom tell Jax or had it been a secret between us?

If Jax knew I was onto him, I might be dead even if my brain wasn't bleeding. I need to play it safe. Molly is missing, and I don't want to put her or Mom in jeopardy any more than I have to. Merely admitting I am from an alternate past or present will put Mom in the line of fire, but I don't have a choice, and part of me, a big part of me, wants to hurt her.

All I wanted was to get to know her, but the more time I spend with her, the more I wish I hadn't. My longing memories of her were better. Now I'm left with only pain, and I don't even have my dad.

Mom licks her lips, about to speak. I steel myself for what's to come, trying to plan my response, but I have no idea what to do. No idea how to protect us all from the horrible truth that we have been living with the same man who tore our family apart the last ten years. I'll have to wing it.

"Jax adopted you," Mom's voice tremors. "You are—"

"That's not what I meant, and I think you know it. I think you've known for a while, haven't you?"

She touches the curls dangling in front of my face and pushes her lips together to quell their trembling, but she doesn't speak, which forces me to.

"You were dead," I whisper, afraid to speak any louder. "I was raised by my father, your widower. He meant everything to me, but I wanted nothing more than to know you, so I took a chance, a big chance, to save you."

She closes her eyes, and tears dribble down her cheeks. "You were the girl in the alley. Shot and disappeared."

I nod. Finally, maybe we can have an honest, real conversation.

"For the last few years, I knew you looked like her." She inhales deeply, her chest rising and falling with the cleansing breath. "... but the last few days even more. Your curls ..." she says, fingering my ringlets.

"She didn't want to look like you anymore."

"No!" Her voice cracks, and I watch the pain, the hurt, etch on her face like shattered glass. "You blamed me for it all, but it hurt me too. John tried to have me killed. I had no choice to provide for us. I didn't pick this life for us and I hate it just as much as you did.."

My nostrils flare. "He isn't guilty. I saw the pain him of losing you, how much he sacrificed to keep us together. Working three jobs, living in a crummy apartment, just so we could get by."

"Then why change the past? Why risk your life?"

"Because I wanted to save you for us. I wanted to know my mother. I wanted us all together. I didn't save you to work or get remarried, that's for sure."

She hangs her head, and I close my eyes as a storm rolls in behind them—the start of a new headache. But it isn't bad, yet.

"What do you expect me to do with this new information?" she whispers. "Thank you? Run to your father? Forget about Molly?"

"I don't know. Stop looking at me like you hate me is a good start."

Her lower lip sticks out. "I don't hate you. For the love of God, Lara." She stands up and paces over to the wall. Leaning against it, her posture crumbles like a mountain collapsing into itself.

"So I was dead?"

I nod. "Shot in that alley."

"And you took the bullet for me?" Mom turns and looks at me. "I'm supposed to be dead, so what the hell am I supposed to do now?" Her hand trembles and covers her mouth, but ekes out a gasp.

I stare down at my hand, waiting, waiting for the ability to tell her how much I love her, but it never seems to come.

"Because your dad wasn't charged doesn't make him innocent. Just because he loved you, doesn't mean he loved me."

"I saw that he did. He kept your pictures. He looked at them when he thought I wasn't watching." I tug on my fingers. "And ... he sent me back in time for my birthday—my first birthday—at that Italian restaurant on 4th. I saw how happy you were."

Surprise spreads across her face, and the first smile I've seen graces her lips. "I forgot about that place. We loved it there. And you ... were such a happy baby."

"I knocked into the waitress. A bunch of stuff fell, and I realized I could touch the past, not like the techs told me."

Mom sucks in her breath, and I see the wheels spinning in her head. She's probably thinking about her research, if I could be one of her test subjects. "So you came back ... to save me. You thought you'd wake up and what, we'd all be living happily ever after?"

I shrug. "Why not? How was I supposed to know someone would frame Dad?"

Mom holds a hand to her chest and takes in a breath that quivers the air between us. "You want to prove him innocent, is that it?" Her eyes blink quickly. "These x-rays prove you're going to die, Lara. Die."

"That's why I have to act fast."

Mom shakes her head. "I've been working on something that can help you. It's risky, but I don't see any other alternative."

"I know what you've been working on, and I know you want out. So you can stop pretending now."

Her eyes bulge, and her hands tremble. "Lara, what you know—"

"Is dangerous, I know."

"Could get you killed!" She takes another deep breath and squeezes her eyes shut. "Who have you told?"

"No one."

"Thank God. We won't have to put up with this much longer. I've made arrangements for all of us, but until then ... we can't tell Jax. We have to get Molly back."

Does Mom know Jax is the one who tried to kill her? "Does the senator have Molly?"

Mom swallows hard. "I don't know. If I knew—"

"But you suspect. You need to tell the police."

"She'll kill Molly," Mom whispers. "I can't."

For once, I agree with her.

"We can't make any moves against her, not while her men have Molly. We have to wait and see what it is she wants. First thing we have to do is get you fixed."

The anger melts away as she embraces me. I haven't forgotten what I said, but it doesn't seem to matter as much now. Her hug is strong and comforting. She wants to take care of everything. I want her to, but I can't let her.

Mom smiles, and I see joy in her eyes. "I feel like I'm seeing you for the first time. I guess I am, in a sense.

She stands and smooths her pants before placing her open palm against my forehead. I think of all the times Dad did that when I was home sick from school, but he never wore worry lines as deep as Mom's are right now. Her eyes are a million miles away, and I know the things that must be running through her head. Molly never should've been born Her life with Jax was never supposed to happen. Was John Crane really innocent?

She bends over and kisses me, her fingers running through my hair. I close my eyes, and to my surprise, all I feel is love. In that moment it makes everything I've done worthwhile. Even if my feelings are wrong, I can't shake them. Having a Mom is all I ever wanted.

"I'll make the arrangements. Get some rest. I'll be back." She heads towards the door.

"Mom? I love you," I say, gripping the sheets.

She nods, and I see the tears are back. "You have no idea."

As she leaves, I close my eyes. I take a few deep breaths and then throw the covers off and rip the oxygen tubes from my nose. Mom's ideas are nice, but I can't sit by with my dad in jail and Molly missing. Her kidnapping is my fault, and in case I don't make it out alive, I have to move fast.

It takes me a few minutes to acclimate to walking. I wobble over to the wardrobe against the wall and find my clothes folded on the bottom. Quickly, I dress and grab the duffle bag from the top shelf. It's embroidered with the words *Mass General Hospital*. I sling it over one shoulder and check the hallway for movement.

Only a few nurses loiter in the halls, and their backs are turned to me. I sneak out and hurry toward the stairs marked *EXIT*." Placing my hand on the door to the stairwell, I connect with a familiar face around the corner from the cafeteria.

Surprise rolls across Jax's face, and he nearly drops the cup of coffee in his hand.

I bite my lip, turn my head, and push the door open before dashing toward the steps.

"Lara!" His scream chases after me. Before I hear the door latch, he reaches the stairwell. "Don't do this, Lara!"

But I am already down half a flight of stairs. I keep charging down the steps as fast as I can without catching my breath until I reach the bottom floor, severely winded. Above me, heavy steps echo with a metallic boom. I can't allow myself to get caught. I can't. I dive through the door into the hospital lobby. People stop to stare, but I keep running toward the glass doors.

"Stop her!" Jax calls out from behind me.

I charge towards the two security guards blocking the open exit. As one tries to grab me, I slip past him and drop to the ground, sliding head first through the open door.

My lungs fill with the fresh morning air as my feet pound the pavement, following the street lights up the hill toward a waiting cab. I pull the back passenger door open and throw myself into the cushions, ensuring my feet are inside before I slam the door shut.

"Drive!"

To his credit, the cabby complies. He glances at me, using the rearview mirror, and I see tired blue eyes and enough scruff on his chin to know he hasn't shaved in at least a few days.

"Mind telling me where we're going?"

"YMCA on Broad Street."

His eyebrows rise. "You have enough cash for that? Long drive."

I hold up my plastic credit card as my response. Yeah, I can afford it.

Chapter Eighteen

I watch the street lights whizz past as the soft melody of a symphony orchestra is pumped through the small cab, soothing and relaxing me. I've messed up royally, which was never more apparent than that afternoon in the mall. I can accept my mistakes. I should have listened to Rick and never changed the past, but now my mom is alive, and I have a brother, a sister. A sister in danger, but maybe if I can prove who kidnapped her, we can get her back unharmed.

Maybe.

It all hinges on whether Jax kidnapped her or arranged it somehow. I pray he is the one that took her because then maybe she will be safe. If it was a stranger, I have nothing to go on, and I'm running out of time.

Then there is my dad, but thinking about him breaks my heart. He would say go after the girl. He always put people above himself. Always.

If I can get the evidence behind Mom's attempted murder, Molly's kidnapping, everything, I can clear Dad, save Molly, and maybe be in time to get treatment for my brain. That last item is less than likely, but I need hope above all else.

The clock is approaching midnight when the cab pulls up to the curb beside the YMCA. The downtown street is busy, but since it's still late at night—early in the morning, depending on your point of view—the cabby pulls right up to the door.

I charge my ride, and he offers me a friendly smile, which I pay no attention to as I climb out of the cab. There's a public service announcement coming over the speakers of the radio, "*Vote Yes on Question 2 if you want police to catch the mugger who stole your purse before he ever stole it. End crime before it begins.*

Arriving at the YMCA door, I give it a solid tug.

It doesn't budge.

Dammit. I shove it and then try pulling again, but the lock refuses to give way. With my hands cupped around my eyes, I peer inside the windows, but I only see a few lights inside. I can't make anyone out at reception, or anywhere else for that matter. Then I notice the decal on the window.

24-hour access.

I tear through my purse—lipstick, a mirror, cell phone, but no keycard. In my wallet I see photos, more plastic than the Barbie aisle at Toys"R"Us, and behind my student ID, the keycard. A state-of-the-art all-access pass. I feel the need to even hide that. It causes a shiver to run up my spine.

After I swipe the card, the door beeps and the lock plate lights up green. I swing the door open and run inside the open reception area. The clinking gym equipment in the distance is punctuated with grunts of men straining with their weights.

I sprint down the hall toward the women's restroom. Inside, the lights almost blind me, but I head on through to find the lockers. I can tell I'm nearing the pool because the chlorine and bleach in the air makes my nose burn.

Locker 63.

My eyes sweep aisle after aisle until I find the one I'm looking for. It's a blue and unassuming, but it could unlock the secret to everything. I lick my lips as I insert the key, close my eyes, and with a prayer, twist.

Click.

The door opens, and inside I find more than documents. There's also pink hoodie, a duffle bag, and a fresh change of clothes.

What was I preparing for? What was I doing? I open the manila envelope on the bottom and flip through the documents—a lot of reports, surveillance photos, old newspaper clippings. I don't have time to go through all of it now, so I stash them in my duffle bag and throw on some new clothes.

A tight-fitting t-shirt, pink hoodie, and comfortable blue jeans are my new outfit. It's a weird choice for trendy, sophisticated Lara, but she was up to something big. Real big.

I lift the hidden duffle bag out of the locker, surprised at how hefty it is. I unzip it and find money inside. A lot of money. I touch it. Must be thousands of dollars bound together in neat little stacks.

My heart quickens as I wonder where it came from and what I was planning to do with it. If ever there was a moment for a flashback, it's now. A shining blue cell phone at the bottom of the duffle bag catches my attention. I pull it out and see a note stuck to it. In my handwriting.

Hide in the shower. Move fast.

Wide eyed and with pounding heart, I slam the locker, grab everything, and run down the hall. I turn into the showers and duck into a stall, the vinyl shower curtain flapping against me. I still it with trembling fingers as I hear heavy steps enter the locker room.

The locker doors are banged in rapid succession as the steps draw closer. I don't know why I'm afraid, but I am. It could be a burnt-out exerciser with their iPod on too loud or a cleaning lady coming to collect towels, but I am sure it isn't. I am sure whoever it is, they are here for me.

My still breath echoes with exasperation in my ringing ears. My hearing feels supercharged, and I imagine the rubber soles stepping onto the wet tile at the entry way of the shower room. My eyes flutter open, and my mouth is frozen as I see a shadow creeping closer behind the shower curtain.

A deep, angry voice calls out. "She was here. She got everything."

Something lands on the floor with a wet thud.

My hospital clothes!

I left them beside the bench. I want to berate myself for being so stupid again, but as the shadow begins to recede, I realize that pile of clothes may have saved my life.

Only after the door slams shut do my shoulders relax, but I don't feel safe enough to come out yet. My mind drifts back to the note. It saved my life, but how did I know to write it? How did I know those men were coming for me?

I ask the question a million times in a million different ways but always come up with the same answer.

I wrote it in the future.

And brought it back into the past.

Chapter Nineteen

Suddenly, I feel a little better. I now know I'm alive in the future and in well enough condition to write a note and find a method of time travel. I guess my brain won't be turned into a vegetable. Somewhere out there, I'm still kicking, at least to the point where I wrote this note.

But why? If I'm still alive, if the men didn't kill me, why risk being exposed by the note? Maybe Molly was killed. Maybe Jax got away with it? Maybe I was kidnapped and everything went to hell in a hand basket. Whatever happened, I have to accept that I might never know and thinking about the what-ifs is only wasting time.

I need to get out of here, find a place to lay low where I can go over the documents until the kidnappers call. I can only think of one place people would never suspect this Lara would go to hide—not her boyfriend's and not her BFF's house, but an old friend. I haven't been to Rick's house in years.

I pull out my new cell phone, afraid the existing one might be traced.

After a few rings, Rick answers. Thank God he didn't ignore the unknown phone number.

"Rick—"

"Lara? Are you okay? You're all over the news."

Reporters. Cameras. I forgot all about them. Good thing I didn't need anything from my house. Boy, would that have been a mess.

"I'm okay." I lie for now. It's not as if I have time to explain everything. "Remember how you said if I needed help with my dad you would be there? Well, I need you, Rick." My voice cracks, and my chin trembles.

After a brief pause that feels more like an hour, he responds, "Come to my apartment. It's the least I can do. Just wait out by the back door, and be quiet."

I nod and end the call. I hope I know what I'm doing. Gripping the phone against my chest, I pray.

I catch a bus because I don't want anyone to trace me to Rick's. When he opens the door, I'm struck by how tired he appears. His eyes lack their usual shimmer. He ushers me inside quietly, and we tiptoe past his parents' room.

His room is almost identical to how I remember it. The bed, the dresser, everything looks the same. My eyes are drawn to the small television balancing on top of his dresser. The volume is turned down low, but the hospital is on the screen with a horde of reporters in the background. I catch a story scrolling in the ticker.

Local Girl Kidnapped. Sister escapes custody from the hospital. Sought by police for questioning.

My heart skips a beat, and I turn to see Rick's eyebrow is arched. "You want to run that *I'm fine* business by me again?"

"I am ... for now. I have stuff to do. I found it, see? " I toss my duffle bags onto his bed.

He glances at the bags, then returns his stare to me. "What's in there?"

"The holy grail of my life. Proof about who killed— tried to kill—my mom. Want to venture a guess?" I can't keep the anger out of my voice.

"Well, I know it isn't me, so who was it?"

"Jax." I can barely stop myself from breaking down. My eyelids flutter, and it's all I can do to keep myself from falling apart.

Rick's eyes seem to widen and contract at the same time. "Your stepdad?"

"One and the same." I lick the corner of my lips. "One and the same," I whisper again, my body going numb.

He guides me over to his bed and helps me sit down. "What are we going to do? What's your plan?"

"Read it over and see what it is. This can free my dad. I know it! But the kidnappers will be calling soon. They want this stuff back."

Rick sighs. "Jax took Molly? That doesn't make any sense."

He's right. It doesn't. I bite my lip as I feel the tremor of a headache, but it's still light enough for me to ignore. "Can you get me some meds? Tylenol?"

Nodding, he goes to his dresser and rummages through the top drawer. He tosses me a bottle of pills, and I swallow them dry. He sits down beside me again on the sofa and pushes back the curls off my shoulder. When his fingers graze my neck, I shiver and feel goose bumps rise off my body.

I gaze at him, wanting to close my eyes, to lean in for that hello kiss. His eyes are deep and penetrating,

I feel he wants to kiss me too, but instead he says, "Should we get started?"

His room is beginning to feel small and hot, so I remove my hoodie and slide down onto the floor. We start looking through the surveillance photos. There's my mom at our apartment, my dad holding my hand on the way to school, Mom meeting someone for lunch at an outdoor café …

Hmmm. I can't see his face, buried behind a potted tree, but they are holding hands across the table, and Mom is smiling. In front of them are two iced teas. I squint and bring the photo closer to my face. Mom isn't wearing her wedding ring. That doesn't make any sense.

My heart gallops, and I fan the black and white photos in front of me. I search for that one perfect photo, the one with the smoking gun proving Jax is the one who wanted to kill my mother. Instead, I find the opposite. They were in love.

Jax, with his blond hair, holds my mother in his arms under an awning. They are in a deep, passionate kiss, and Mom grips him as if her life depends on it. It proves what they told me, but it also proves someone else knew and that someone had been following them.

If they were having an affair, why would he want her dead? And why frame my father? Is it possible I remembered wrong? Maybe Jax didn't try to kill her after all. Maybe I'm trying to piece together something that makes sense for my desires, something simple, cut and dry. I have no idea what is real or imagined anymore.

"Did this come out in the trial?" I ask.

Rick nods. "You don't remember?"

I glare at him.

"It came out your mother had an affair. They said your dad hired a private investigator to follow her and take photos to prove it."

That can't be right. Dad wouldn't have done that. My stomach sinks like a rock.

Rick sits down at his computer and boots it up. Is this the right time for him to check his email?

"What are you doing?" I ask, unable to get the edge off of my voice.

"Looking up the court transcripts."

"You can do that?"

"They're all public record."

Oh, I think, but don't say anything quite so stupid aloud. I listen to Rick's typing and close my eyes, allowing my mind to drift away. Rick breaks the silence, chattering excitedly. "Got it. I thought I remembered my parents talking about this. Your dad claimed he never paid for a private investigator, but a money trail convinced them that money went from your dad to the P.I. Your dad exploded in court and said he was being setup, that Rewind and Jax wanted him out of the way. But there was never any proof he was right. Fifteen minutes later he was held in contempt."

"Everyone thought he was lying," I say, void of emotion. I cross my arms.

"Yeah." He turns to face me, his eyes searching mine. "You're sure he's innocent? Really sure? Because it looks like ..."

"I know what it looks like," I say, hoarse. I take a deep breath, my chest trembling. I think about the pictures I've seen against the backdrop of what I know of a man who loved me so completely he worked three jobs, never took a vacation, and never complained other than to say he wanted to spend more time with me.

I threw everything I had away without a second thought. I have no choice but to say, "Absolutely. You or some lame internet document can't change my mind."

"Okay, okay." he says, puffing out his chest. "I get it, Lara. I do. Just ... had to make sure."

"Can you find out more about the financial documents they are talking about?"

Another piece clicks in my brain.

I recall my last flashback, the one when I first snooped inside Jax's office and found the files. I remember making sure to find and print the financial documents.

Dumping the rest of the papers on the floor, I fan them out, thumbing through them all. Finally, I see a computer printout and hold it up. It seems I highlighted an entry.

From ten years ago.

It shows money from Rewind's account being transferred to a private bank. According to my notes in the margin, the account number was linked to an offshore account. My writing is frenzied, sporadic, and I can tell I was excited, but how did I link that account number to my dad?

Maybe I don't need the answer. Maybe the police can do it for me. It's time to bundle up the documents and take them there. But what about Molly?

If I can make a copy, maybe I can do both—give a copy to the kidnapper and the originals to the police? I need to get to a copy machine fast. Plus, there is still the little issue of the flash drive in my pocket.

Argh. I need to get Molly and her locket, but how am I going to keep the flash drive away from the kidnappers? How?

Of course, however I do this, I'll most likely be exposed, but at least my dad will be able to appeal his conviction. Hopefully, Molly will be released, and those guys who were on my trail and wanted me dead, with any luck, will go away once I'm under police protection. No matter what happens to me, at least the truth will be known and everything will be set right, at least as right as I can make it. I put everything back into my bag and swing it over my shoulder.

"Rick …"

He holds his hands up. "Don't say anything. Let's get you where you need to go."

Before we can get down the hall, the doorbell rings, followed by door-rattling knocking. Rick's parents' bedroom lights up down the hall. He shoves me into the linen closet and follows suit, closing it shut behind us. In the tight space, my back pushes up against a shelf that smells like vanilla lavender, while my front is dangerously close to Rick. The scent of his aftershave makes me want to touch him even worse. We are so close I can practically feel his heartbeat and I can definitely see a vein throbbing in his neck.

In the hall, footsteps rush toward the front door and whomever is pounding on it.

"You have any damn idea what time it is?" says the gruff, recently awoken voice of Rick's father. I picture the burly man with his arms crossed.

"Looking for Lara Crane Montgomery. Is she here?"

I recognize the voice from the YMCA. How did they track me down? My heart leaps wildly, wedged in my throat, and I can't swallow as the ringing in my ears intensifies. I shake my head at Rick, begging him to stay quiet.

"Lara? Lara moved away from here a long time ago. Rick hasn't been friends with her in years."

"We have reason to believe she's been in contact with him. If we could take a look around—"

"You'll do no such damn thing. I don't see no badges or warrants, and unless you're the police, you have no right to come in here or be looking for that girl."

"We need to return her to the hospital. She's a sick girl."

My eyes squeeze shut. Part of me still can't accept this, can't believe it. A tremor starts to form in my arms, but Rick quells it by squeezing my hands in his. I see compassion and fear in his eyes. Neither of us is sure what's about to happen .

"I saw the horrible stuff going on with her sister on the news. Still doesn't change the fact we haven't seen her in years, and you're not getting in this house. Now, before I call the cops—"

"We're leaving."

The man huffs, and not a second later, the door slams shut, rattling the knocker and echoing vibrations through the apartment. Inside me though, the vibration can't be quelled. Waves of relief flow through me, and I take a deep, calming breath.

Rick too relaxes his shoulders, but his hands still hold mine. We wait to hear that his dad has gone back to bed, and then we sneak out of the closet and race as quiet mice back to his bedroom.

While he quietly latches the door and dims the lights, I glance outside and see some men loitering near a van. A glowing cigarette ember drifts into one of their hands. With the use of some old bird-watching binoculars, I can see they are all dressed in black, wearing fine watches, and have tattoos on their hands, except for one guy who also has one on the back of his neck. He's tall, blond, and bears a striking resemblance to Mr. Clean.

These men look tough. I don't think I've ever felt so much fear. I have no idea how I'm going to get out without being seen.

Their tattoos seem familiar. I try to think where I might have seen them before, but the deeper I think, the more my headache intensifies. I realize I don't remember, but Lara—the old one I am slowly merging into, does.

I slide down on the floor beneath the window to try to relax, to let the image come, but Rick kneels before me.

"Lar? You okay?" He strokes my hair back. Is he finally going to kiss me? Maybe he realizes we're meant to be together. "Your eyes are going bloodshot. Lara? Can you hear me?"

My jaw presses firmly together, and as his strong, warm hands grip the sides of my face, the image zooms into view with a pop.

****

I'm standing at the front door of my house holding a ladle. I'm wearing a small apron covering my midriff, and I have one hand on the doorframe. On the other side of the threshold are four men, all in black suits, all with matching tattoos. They scare me, but I put on a brave face and pretend otherwise.

"Can I help you?" I try to keep my voice balanced.

One of them steps forward, bald with a gleaming head and wearing dark shades. He clasps his hands in front of each other, revealing a gold ring with a diamond, but he doesn't seem the marrying type.

"Are your parents home?"

"Not yet," I say coolly. "But I have friends over, so I need to go."

"Don't have time to play twenty questions, is that it?" The man smirks. Maybe he knows he's making me uncomfortable.

"That's right. I'm making dinner for the kids, so if you don't mind …" He catches the door in the palm of his thick hand.

"Tell Jax we stopped by, would you?" His smile reveals a fake gold tooth as I close the door and latch it.

My limbs are shaking, and I lean against the door, able to feel someone move beside me. Donovan puts his hand on my shoulder. His eyes are worried as I stare up into them.

"It was him," I say grimly, and Donovan takes me readily into his arms.

I feel safe, safer than I have in months as I wrap my arms around him and cry into his shoulder. He strokes my hair and kisses my cheek.

"Prom better hurry up and get here," he says. "Are you sure this is what you want?"

I nod. I've never been so sure in all my life. First, I get the proof, and then I travel back to the day my dad was framed.

And expose them all.

Chapter Twenty

Prom.

I'm a fool.

Donovan and Lara were using it as a cover to go back in time. One of them was going to use their parents' credentials to sneak in and use the time travel equipment. Once Lara knew everything she needed, she would stop her father from being framed and expose the future senator, Jax, and Rewind. She was going to blow the lid off them all and use their own technology to do it. What a brilliant girl.

But did Donovan know? I suspect not if he was acting so blasé about it. I need to keep it that way. If he was going to be my ally, he couldn't know what his mom had done.

The love I felt in Donovan's arms stays with me as Rick's face comes into view. His face, the one I love, is confused with my feelings for Donovan. It was a small but powerful vision, and I can understand now, if we were planning this giant event behind everyone's back, why he's been so angry with my behavior. I pretty much destroyed this guy's life with a single, selfish act. Everything I did up until Molly went missing was selfish. I stole my mom back from time, and now time wants retribution, starting with my brain.

Rick licks his lips, waiting for me to speak. "What'd you see?"

"Donovan. He … knows these guys. I think he can help me."

I fish the phone out of my duffle bag. Donovan's number is the only one in speed dial. He must be the one who gave it to me, so we could contact each other without being tracked.

It only takes half a ring for Donovan to answer. "Thank God. I've been waiting for you to call. And then when I saw the news?"

"I'm at Rick's. I have the papers." My eyes stay on Rick, watching for an expression.

"Rick's?" There's no denying the anger in his voice.

"I didn't want anyone to find me. Nothing happened."

Jesus, Lara—"

"I know." I check to see the van still parked out front. Bad news. "The men are here. I need to find a way out."

He exhales again. "Okay, okay. Let me think ... If there's a back exit, use it in twenty. Give me some time to get there. How far is the nearest Dunkin' Donuts?"

"There's one on every corner. There's one on Lincoln."

"Perfect, meet me there. At this time of night, where there's donuts, there will be cops. As a safety precaution."

"So what? You think they're going to try to snatch me or something?"

"If they're following you—tracking you—that's exactly what they're going to do. Leave Rick there. We don't need any additional baggage."

I realize he's right, and I nod before ending the call. As Rick draws the curtains shut, I stand, ready to say goodbye. It could be for forever, but I don't want to say that. "Till next time," I say with a small smile and extend my hand.

Rick stares at it like it's an insult and hugs me instead. "Be careful."

His voice is filled with darkness. I think he knows how dangerous it is, and he doesn't ask to come. It's odd because my Rick would do anything for me, but this one, he's not in love with me. He might sense our attraction, but it's not the real deal. That notion tastes like bitter coffee.

I feel his arms tighten around me. I rest my head on his shoulder, in my mind saying goodbye to him for good, but when I open my eyes I see under his bed.

An open duffle bag, overflowing with money.

I push away. Suddenly, everything in me is saying I need to get away. It's not safe.

"I'll see myself out." His hand clamps my shoulder.

"Nonsense. I'll make sure the coast is clear."

When I look into his face, I know there's no wiggle room. He's angry and will never let me go without a fight. We sneak out of the apartment, and he gently closes the door behind us. I gawk at him as he takes the duffle bag from me and we start walking down the cramped hallway.

"I can carry that myself," I say, reaching for the handle. I pull the hoodie over my head as we pass by several kids idling in the halls, an old radio pumping out tunes. "What are you doing, Rick?"

"Making sure you get out safe." He grips my arm much too tight.

"You're hurting me."

I grit my teeth and yank, but he won't let me go. His face has gone icy cold and his features drawn flat. I can read nothing in him.

Was everything at my house, the mall a lie?

He pulls me down the stairs towards the men from the van, who are coming to meet us. I throw a glance over my shoulder and see the kids from the hall also coming toward us. One is holding a crow bar. The other a gun. Fear builds. It's all I can feel.

"You set me up. For what? Money!"

As the backdoor crashes open, Rick wraps his arms around my torso and squeezes hard. I gasp for air and kick my legs as he lifts me.

"Money might not be anything to you. You've had it most of your life. But to me? It can change everything for me and my family. Everything!"

Did he ever believe me about the time travel? I can't be sure, but it's clear he is not the Rick I knew. The Rick I was in love with, who would never do anything like this. Never.

I try to use my legs to catch the door frames, but the men grab them. I lean my head to the side to scream, but a cloth is pressed to it. I try to suck in air, but a harsh chemical odor stings my senses. I start coughing as I'm thrown into the back. The door is latched before I can get to my knees. Someone smacks the roof, and the van takes off like a rocket, knocking me down.

The vibration rocks my butt. Everything in the back of the van begins to double. I see two blankets instead of one. Two bags of rice instead of one. I have four hands instead of two.

Not only did those bastards drug me, but Rick helped them.

Chapter Twenty-One

I'm gone, lost in a memory as vivid as a dream. Back at my house, in the living room, I sit on the sofa beside Donovan. I'm wearing a fancy yet understated dress, and his arm is draped across my shoulder. Pink streamers decorate the living room, and a few stray balloons are hung by the fireplace. Sitting to our left and right are Donovan's parents, Joseph and Patricia James, and to my left is Jax.

I watch him as he leans forward and scoops some crackers from the coffee table. I'm barely able to force a smile as our eyes meet. His hold a question he wouldn't dare ask when his boss is around.

"Can I get you another drink, Joe? Senator?" Jax asks.

Patricia holds up her hand with a smile. "Please, call me Pat while I'm out of Washington. And no, I'm fine. Being in your fine home again is enough."

"To the birthday girl, eh?" Joseph says and raises his half-empty glass.

I nod my thanks and accept the fruit punch offered by Mom before she bustles back into the kitchen. I can smell that the roast beef is almost done—my favorite.

"I'm glad you could come," Joseph continues. "Don always has high praises for both of you."

"What can I say? I'm a chip off the old block, right Dad?"

I can't help but laugh. He always makes things better. His dimples are cute, and I wish we could be alone. When I look back at his parents, they are smiling at me.

My eyes settle on Patricia, whose eyes flash something other than happiness at me. I force a smile and pretend everything is all right.

"Oh, look at them, Joe," she gushes, patting her husband's knee. "A perfect couple. I'm sorry we haven't done this before. You know, Washington is a slave driver."

"I bet," I say, sipping my punch.

Jax laughs and gestures at Joseph. "So is this man. The guy has been my boss for years, and he still surprises me with the workload."

Joseph crosses his arms and chuckles. "You get to leave early every night to take care of your family. I don't see what you have to complain about. Your wife on the other hand …"

The doorbell rings, and Jax excuses himself to answer it. I'm curious; no one else was invited tonight. I follow him out to the hall where Mom meets me. She's wiping her hands on her apron.

"Who is it, Jax?" Mom asks. Jax blocks the door and whispers to someone. "Who is it, Dad?" I ask louder.

He turns around, wiping the corner of his lips. His cheeks are beet red and sweat clings to his brow. I've never seen him so nervous about anything.

"My brother Rex is in from London, it would seem, and has dropped by."

"Brother?" I have never heard of a brother before.

Mom smiles and extends her hand as Rex enters. He's tall, the spitting image of Jax except for his black hair and brown eyes. I don't bat an eye at his showing up, but my future self knows different.

I didn't see Jax in the alley. Jax didn't kill my mother.
Rex did.

And now he's back. Has he come to complete the job? Or is something far worse going on?

"A pleasure to meet you." Mom kisses his cheek.

He is all smiles, and everything about him—his smile, his accent, even his suit is smooth. Like honey and butter, only over processed and sickeningly sweet. "Lovely to finally to see you in person. Your pictures do not do you justice at all." His voice is thick with a British accent. He kisses Mom's hand.

She almost seems wooed by him, but then Rex does a double take when he spots me.

Nervously, I take a step backwards as he offers me his hand.

"And would this be the lovely, Lara? Well, you are grown up, aren't you?"

I shake his clammy hand.

"Dad never …" My voice trails off when my eyes lock with Jax. His are afraid, nervous. I don't know why he's so scared, but I don't think Rex is friendly. No matter if he's my uncle or not, I don't want him in our house.

"Yes, Jax and I, we've had a few falling outs over the years, but we are working on mending our fences, aren't we brother?" Rex clasps Jax on the shoulder, and I sense he would rather be anywhere but here.

I want to ask why. As I'm thinking about it, Mom speaks up. "Help set the table, Lara. Rex, you can stay for dinner?"

He smirks. "Oh, I wouldn't dream of missing it. Tell me where I can find Mike and Molly. So delighted to hear twins really do run in the family."

The twins are thrilled to find out they have a British uncle. They spend most of the dinner asking him to say certain words or phrases and asking about British slang. It amuses Mom, but Jax never cracks a grin. He barely touches his dinner.

"Tell me about your work, senator? Is it true you're looking to loosen the laws on time travel?" Rex asks.

Joseph chuckles. "Has been for years!"

Patricia swallows carefully and picks up her glass of wine. "It would seem to me we are wasting a valuable resource. Don't have time to go on a vacation? Borrow a memory from someone who did. You'll spend a fraction of the time in the chair but wake refreshed."

"And three times as much money," Donovan cracks.

Everyone laughs, but Rex points at him. "Money makes the world go round, doesn't it? Certainly it does. What does the government think about time travel to save the world?"

Patricia smiles, sits up straighter, and with confidence says, "Soon, if I have my way, that's exactly how it will be. I hope to have enough votes to pass a law that ensures the police have the real power they need."

Mom and Patricia clink their glasses together. Usually she hates this line of speculation but is good friends with the senator, which is how Donovan and I met.

Jax's eyes are far off. I don't think he's hearing anything that's going on at all.

Rex plays with his butter knife. "So the world will be made safer, thanks to you then? Murderers will be taken out before they commit crimes, rapists, kidnappers, all of them erased?"

"Can't happen. For one, if you try to change the past, your mind will turn to mush. We want them stopped, rehabilitated, not dead," Mom says. "Second, what you're talking about is murder."

"What's a little casual murder among friends," Rex says, eyeing me specifically.

I shift in my seat, sitting up straighter and trying to act as if he's not bothering me.

"That's why we have the memories, isn't it?" Patricia says. "If we can take a serial killer and strip his memories from him—his rotten childhood—and insert happy ones, we can quell the instincts, change lives. That is what Miranda is working on."

All eyes fall to my mother, whose jaw is set tight.

"Really, I was unaware your research was so cutting edge?" Rex says.

She gulps back her wine. "I don't talk about this in front of the children. Lara, please start clearing the table."

To be asked to clear the table on your birthday is probably considered by most to be rude, but I am pretty happy about it. I take some dishes into the kitchen and begin to scrape the leftovers into the garbage disposal.

I hear a shuffling behind me and turn to see Rex standing there with his hands in his pockets. "Can I get you something?"

He approaches me and stands so close that I back up into the counter. His eyes search mine. They are deep, penetrating and don't leave my face. I will myself not to blink, but it's not easy.

"You don't know who I am, do you?" he whispers, stroking my hair.

I shake my head. "Should I?"

"You will. I liked the curls better," he says with malice. I don't take another breath until he's gone.

Chapter Twenty-Two

Rex was the assassin.

He had a working relationship with the senator, and even though they pretended not to know, each other, if you knew what to look for, you could see it. Rex tried to kill Mom, and when he failed, she stayed with Rewind and married Jax.

Did Jax know? Was he innocent?

I don't want to hurt him, but I know I need to expose them all.

****

My eyes snap open, and I suck in a sharp intake of air. I'm in a small room surrounded by cement walls with a window far up, but little light is streaming inside. The room is empty except for a mattress I'm lying on.

Pushing up on my elbows, my stomach sways back and forth. I groan and check all my pockets for my phone. It's gone. My legs wobble when I try to stand, and I fall against the wall. I brace myself against it to get to the door, but there's no window and no handle. It is completely flat.

I'm trapped.

My heart is pounding with fear. There's no way out.

Footsteps echo outside. Someone's coming. I look around for a weapon, anything, but the room is barren. Instead, I crouch down in the corner and wait for the door to open.

The men who kidnapped me enter, holding Jax between them. The one with the dragon tattoo throws him to the ground. "Say what needs to be said. Time is short."

He cringes in pain, and I scurry over to him. His face is black and blue, and he's bleeding above one eye. My heart pounds to see him hurt. I grip him by the shoulders, my head collapsing against his chest. The door latches.

We're alone.

Jax's hand rubs the top of my head. "This is all my fault, Lara. I'm sorry. I thought I could control it. Then Molly ..."

His face contorts with pain, but he doesn't cry. He remains strong.

And that helps me stay strong too. "Are you going to hurt me?"

Jax shakes his head. "Never. Never. God, that you think that—of course why would think anything different?" He exhales. "I've made a mess out of everything, Lara. Everything."

I bit my lip and feel like I can trust him. I can see the despair on his face as his rubs his eyes with his hands. He looks like he's living a nightmare. I ask a question I need an answer to even though I'm afraid.

"Did you know Rex was going to try to kill Mom? Did you help him?"

He shakes his head as I help him sit up. "It wasn't like that."

"Tell me," I spit out. "I deserve the truth."

"It started with late nights, dinners ... then dancing. I was in love with your mother, and she—"

"Was married, I know. Then what?"

He leans his head back and looks up at the lights. "You missed your mom. So did John. Miranda was going to quit, spend more time with you, but Patricia James ... wouldn't stand for it. Your mom knew too much about the illegal research, about the illegal money Patricia was funneling into the company when it was a startup."

"The guys who grabbed us, the one with the tattoo, that would make them—"

Jax nods. "Mob. They are invested in your mom's research and keep Patricia on a short leash. Even now, if it got out … they own her. Once, she was our friend, but now … no. She can't be trusted."

"So she hired your brother to take her out?"

Jax's shoulders round, and his face despairs. "I didn't know, not before he took the shot. You have to believe me. We might be brothers, but our lives took very different paths. He was in the mob as an enforcer at a young age, and since then … let's say his skills have improved, all right?"

I do believe him. I see the agony in his face as he talks about his brother. "But you covered it up. You framed my father."

"I didn't have a choice. The mob … they would've tried again. They would've killed your mom, you, me, everyone. But he's my brother. We worked out a deal. He'd never come back. He'd leave us alone … if I kept Miranda at her job, doing her research. If I'd keep her quiet." He takes a deep sigh. "Then we got married. I never thought —"

"You fell in deep." I bite my lip. "You had the twins."

Jax nods.

"So what changed? Why did Rex come back?"

Jax shakes his head. "The senator did. Your mother did. Their relationship … was getting worse. Your mom was going to leave and blow the lid off the whole thing. I didn't know any of this until Molly was taken, until you went missing. But your mom told me about the senator's threats, about what happened to that reporter. Somehow, she had a source and—"

"I'm the source." I watch disbelief roll over his face.

"What? How?"

"I stole proprietary information from Rewind, from Mom, and handed it off to the reporter. They got it back when they killed her. I have it all on video. I can end this if I can get out."

Jax closes his eyes and takes a deep breath. "And Molly? They took her to …"

"Blackmail me, get their stuff back. Seems like it worked." I take a breath to force myself to slow down. "We're all going to die, aren't we?"

"No!" I almost believe him. "No."

"Jax—"

"Listen, I'm sorry for what I did, but I did the best I could."

"What you did …"

"You think I don't know what you're going to say?" Jax narrows his eyes, and his hand caresses my cheek. "Every year, I love you both more. Every year, I see how much harder it is for you. Every year, I feel worse than I did before."

"Every year," I whisper, and my mind flashes back to my father's birthday party.

I scraped birthday cake on top of an unopened envelope. The seal was a golden *M* for Montgomery. And Dad never opened it because he knew who it was from— Mom's lover. He sent us what? A card? Money? Because his brother was responsible and he got away with it.

"You okay?" Jax asks.

"Yeah … a lot to take in."

"Can you forgive me for what I've done?"

I swallow.

He waits silently.

"It might be too much." His face is crestfallen. "But you raised me. I wish you found another way."

185

His lip quivers. "Me too. Do what they say, Lara, then maybe we'll all get out of here, all get a second chance."

I doubt that's true, but I hope it is.

The door opens again and in walks Rex. He looks different than he did the last time I saw him. A scab runs down the side of his face. It looks fresh.

I snarl. "What happened to your face?"

"You did."

My eyebrows furrow. "I think I'd remember," I say, even though it's quite possible I don't.

He crouches down, and his smile is chilling, unkind. "You will later. Just proves our plans for you were successful. You are the one Miranda has been searching for her entire career. How ironic."

I can't fathom what he's talking about. Is he talking about her work?

"I'm sorry, my darling. There's no time to explain. The procedure room is ready for you."

"Rex." Jax glances up at his brother with wide eyes. "You said you'd let her go once you had everything that was yours."

"Plans change." Rex signals his thugs, who grab my arms, forcing me to my feet.

"Let her go!" Jax screams.

I kick my legs and fight them every step of the way. "Let me go!" I pull on my arms and throw my head around. I do everything I can.

Still, they bring me down a long corridor into a sterile room. In the center is a long leather chair, something like a dentist's chair, but with a hole in the headrest. I'm slammed into it and their strong bodies hold me still as they cuff me in.

I scream, thrash, and even manage to bite one of their ears.

"Ahhh!" He backhands me across the jaw.

"Enough!"

My chest heaves as everyone stands to attention. It's Patricia James in a blue executive suit, not a hair out of place. She's the perfect picture of a Washington powerhouse.

She studies me. I've never seen anyone so unwaveringly unapologetic, but I've never been kidnapped before.

"Have you forgotten we have Molly?"

I swallow hard. Part of me did.

"What do you want?" My teeth grit together.

"A weapon. A time traveler. Someone who can get me everything I need to turn around this pathetic country. And according to your brain scans at the hospital ..." Her sneer gives me shivers. "You're it."

I take a deep breath. My insides are shaking.

"You could still die, but this is the only way to save Molly, Jax, your mother. Understood?" She crosses her arms like a school teacher waiting for me to turn in my homework.

Under her penetrating gaze, I nod, but my mind spins. I need to find a way out of this.

"Good. We can be friends if you do what you're told."

I sneer. "Some friend."

"Hmph!"

The next sight turns my blood cold. Men enter the room with my mom between them and slams her onto the floor. A thug places his hand on her neck, keeping her down in place.

"I won't do this to my daughter. I won't!" she cries out.

I squeeze my eyes shut and lean my head back. Everything I went through to save her, and now she's back in danger no matter what else I do. Maybe that's how things are. Maybe I have no control. Maybe I can't save her. But I don't believe it for one second. Mom *can* be saved. We all can, if I can only figure out how.

I must go through with my old plan, go back in time to when this all started. If I catch Rex at the scene and turn him in, this future won't exist.

It's my only shot.

"You saw the brain scans," Patricia says. "This is the only thing that might save her life. You have no choice. Or should I get Molly in here?"

"No!" Mom shouts. "Leave her out of this." She stands up and rests a hand on my shoulder. "I'm sorry about this. I'm so sorry, Lara."

I swallow hard. "It's the only way out. Do it."

Her eyes cloud over. I am the next test subject. They want to unlock time travel in someone, and I am the best candidate. What Patricia doesn't know is I am her worst enemy, and if this works, I'll take her down.

"This is going to hurt," Mom says.

I open my eyes and try not to look as she readies a needle. I bite my lip as she slides it into the base of my skull.

When she pulls it out, I gasp for air, my fingers gripping at the arm rest.

"Mom?" I whisper, my lips trembling.

She's holding a metal hose in her hand and begins to fish it through the back of the chair. I can't see much, which makes my heart palpitate. I can barely keep still and am beginning to sweat.

"I love you, baby," she whispers and leans over to kiss my cheek. "If this works, you need to save Molly. You need to find a way."

I barely nod. I don't want the senator to see.

The tube is attached to my skull, and a moment later searing heat and ice race through my body. My vision flashes to white, then a spectrum of colors.

Agony!

My back arches, my head throws back, and I scream.

After a lifetime of misery, in my mind I see the entrance to an apartment complex. My finger hovers over the buzzer for 302c.

The label reads *Joyce Meyers*.

Chapter Twenty-Three

The young woman who answers the door of 302c has blonde hair, cut simply, but stunning eyes. So this is Joyce Meyers. I nervously walk in and hand her the duffle bag.

She examines the contents. "This is everything?"

I cross my arms and pace. Being there is my goal, but it's making my skin crawl. "Yes. Do you think it'll be enough?"

"To free your father? I don't know, but to get an inquiry into Rewind and the senator? Absolutely. I'll look over everything and get back to you as soon as I can."

I smile at her as she places a hand on my shoulder. We stop short of the front door as the doorbell rings.

"Are you expecting someone?" I ask.

She runs to peer through the peephole. "Quick, hide!"

I grab the duffle bag and run. Frantic, I slam myself into the linen closet, barely able to catch my breath.

I hear voices, one of them familiar. Fishing my cell phone out of my pocket, I start recording a video. Through the slats in the door, I can make out Joyce. Her mouth is slack and her eyes wide as she raises her hands up in self-defense. The thug with the neck tattoo clamps a cloth over her mouth. She struggles and then goes limp in their arms.

I cover my mouth to keep from screaming. He lays her down on the ground and another face comes into few. Patricia James.

"Make it look like a suicide this time."

This time."

I turn off my phone and squeeze my eyes shut, shoving it into my pocket as I kneel down so no one will see me. If they catch me, I'm dead, but this video might be what I need to stop the senator for good.

"Find the evidence. Find out who her source is."

I only hope they won't find me. Please don't search the closet.

They go to search the bedroom first, so I take the opportunity to peek out of the closet door and look around. The coast is clear. I sling the bag carefully over my shoulder, and with shaking legs I am at the front door in only a few steps. The run down the hall seems to go on forever.

I hear a voice far off. "Whoever she is, get her."

I squeal and hit all the buttons on the elevator before I run down the stairs. I hope they didn't see me.

I hope.

****

I have no idea how much time has passed when I open my eyes next. My body is on fire. The muscles in my arms and legs are shaking from utter exhaustion. Groaning, I roll over in the bed I'm in. It's a hospital bed, but the room is anything but medical. Other than myself and the bed, the room is empty. When I try to sit up, my vision spins like a kaleidoscope. I mash my hands to my eyes and hear the door open.

"Feeling better?" It's the senator. She throws a bag down on my leg. "Financials, schematics. It's all here but one thing."

My eyes flutter open and I glance down. It's my bag, the one with all the evidence in it. I can't look at her. I know what's coming.

"Where is the video?" Anger begins to seep into her voice.

"The video is there."

"Not the one of my conversation with that damn reporter."

"You mean the one when you killed her?" My eyes open and I grin. "Oops."

She grips my arm and bares her teeth. "Where is it! I am not playing games with you or your family."

"No? You think I ever expect I'll get out of here? My mom? You'll never let us go. I've seen enough movies to know we are too big a risk for you. We'll all be framed or disposed of, so I see no reason to help you."

I lay my head back and close my eyes to settle my rolling stomach. "If I am not released, if I don't call your son, he will release the video to the media," I lie, hoping it will buy me some time.

"You told my son?" Her voice is a hushed whisper. "He wouldn't believe you."

"No? Maybe you should ask him."

Patricia backs out the door.

I hope Donovan will be all right. I'm sure he'll piece together what his mom is up to, but I can't bet on it. Somehow, I have to get out of this room and find Molly. If I can get the microchip and release the contents, the senator will be arrested. It's the only way to save me and my family.

****

"I can't," I say.

I groan, my back arching in pain. Electrodes are fastened against my temples, and I am strapped back in the chair. Overhead, the lights grow brighter. The intensity pounds painfully into my brain, but I can't even move my head to get away from them.

"Again." The senator grits her teeth.

Rex is at the controls. I see him shift a gear, and the pain in my head magnifies.

I see a hallway, the one leading to my prison cell, but I resist using time travel. If I show them what I can do, all will be lost. The senator will never leave me alone. She'll make sure I'm never able to go back and fix my mistakes.

I groan again under the strain. My teeth chatter together, and saliva forms at the corner of my mouth. Part of me is drawn, pulled from my body, but I restrain myself. I grip the armrest, refusing to give in. It's like the ultimate staring contest, but the more I hold steady and refuse to give in, the more it hurts, the more my body wants to blink.

"Enough!" Mom screams, trying to force her way past the mob thugs that watch us every step of the way. "She's in pain. She can't do it."

"You better hope she does."

The thug with the golden dragon tattoo says, "If she doesn't, I have the authority to get rid of any loose ends. And you, your family, you're all a loose end."

I can't see what Mom is doing, but I hear the fear in her voice. "Let me give her something. She can't think like this, how is she supposed to do anything in this much pain? Give me a few minutes, please."

"You have five minutes, the senator says. "After that, we will need to see results, Miranda."

A few moments later, a door latches behind us. Mom pushes a few buttons, and the machine restraints loosen. The tension in my head is gone, like a released vaccum seal. My mouth falls open, and I gasp for breath as Mom injects me with something.

"Mom?" I whisper with everything left in me.

"Oh baby." She strokes my forehead. "We have to figure out a way to give them what they want."

I shake my head. "That would be signing your death warrant, and then they'd never leave me alone. I need to fix this. I need to fix it now, Mom."

Her eyebrows furrow. "How can you?"

"Time travel." I give her a tired smile.

Her face drops. "But you can't. You've been at it for hours."

"I haven't been trying. I've been trying not to time travel."

Her hand grips mine. "It might ... it might kill you."

"It might not. If I don't get this right, I'm as good as dead anyway."

She wipes the tears off her cheeks. "You're stronger than me, Lara. I don't know how you've held it together this long, but I love you. Please be careful."

That was always my intent.

"Where will you try to go?"

"I don't know."

I close my eyes and take a deep breath. It's time to try again. The pain is returning with a vengeance. Each blink is like sandpaper, and my tongue is as dry as the desert. If only I hadn't been caught by Rick. If only I had found another way.

The room begins to spin and shift in front of me. The walls, the floor, everything moves in a circle except for me. I am stationary.

"What the?"

My heart races, and I grip the armrest of the bed as everything falls away. I float through darkness, space until my feet land on earth. Air fills my lungs, and everything falls in place around me, brick by brick, almost as if I were inside a LEGO model. A door and then some lights appear. I'm back in the hallway outside Rick's apartment, standing beside myself.

But she is frozen like a mannequin and doesn't seem to see me.

Somehow, I've gone back in time. My mom's experiment worked. The senator was right when she said it was me all along. My headache clears as Rick appears beside me, but he's also frozen in stone. For a brief, moment I peer up into his frozen face.

"I'm sorry," I whisper and yank my duffle bag from his hand.

When the music begins to blare behind us, Rick's face snaps to life. Without waiting for the confusion to clear, I sprint out the door. The air is cool as it greets my face. My legs pump, and my arms swing. I'm in for the run of my life.

Rick chases after me. "Wait!"

I hurry past the van and make a break for the curb. Shielding my eyes, I hear movement to my side and then gunfire. I leap to the ground, ducking behind a light post and an old newspaper vending machine for cover. I look up at the glowing Dunkin' Donuts sign covered in a dream-like fog. It shatters under a hailstorm of bullets.

I cover my head as a set of tires squeal. Donovan's sports car pulls up on the curb to cover me. I dive into the passenger seat, my head down low and scream, "Go!"

Donovan peels away from the curb in a 180 and drives back the way he came. His eyes stay on the road, but his hand squeezes mine. "You all right?"

I nod and clutch the duffle bag to my chest. "Keep driving."

"Where?" His eyes flash from the road to me.

"Police station. I need you to drop all this stuff off in case I don't return."

Anxiety creeps into his voice. "Return? Return from where?"

"The past."

"Lara, you're not making any sense."

"I know, and I'm sorry." I bite my lip. "There's no time to explain. I need to fix all of this so my dad was never framed and Molly was never kidnapped, and there's only one way to do that. I need to go back to the beginning."

Donovan drives under an old abandoned bridge. He cuts the engine and turns to me. His eyes study me, and I study him because I'm afraid the next time I see him, he won't love me at all.

"How do we do that? Do we need to get into Rewind?"

I shake my head and stroke his cheek. "Not anymore."

The features of his face are drawn together. "You never make things dull, you know that?"

I laugh and lean over. In the background, sirens wail and I heard a rush of footsteps. "Remember me when I'm gone."

"Don't talk like this. I could never forget you, Lara."

When our lips meet, the moment is magical. I feel warm everywhere in the blanket of his love, understanding, and compassion. My mind opens up, and suddenly I remember everything.

Everything.

I wish to stay with him forever. I grip his jacket, and his arms squeeze me tight.

But in my mind, I see an alley.

Chapter Twenty-Four

I only had fifteen minutes.

That was how I created the incredible mess that is now my life, but I can fix it.

I need to.

I step out onto the crosswalk. I see the alley, and I see myself get shot. I watch my body crumble.

Mom screams and falls to her knees. "Oh my God," she whispers, throwing glances over her shoulder. "Help! Someone help us!"

"You're going to be okay," she says to me as I lie supposedly dying but really only phasing. "You'll be okay."

I remember how it felt, but I can't pay attention to them as a crowd gathers. I tune out their screams and questions as my eyes focus on Rex. He's running from the alley toward the dumpsters and the chain link fence at the back. I take off sprinting, pushing through the crowd and shoving people out of my way. I jump over my fallen body.

"Hey!" my mom screams, but I don't think she notices how much I look like the girl she is tending to.

Good.

I keep going, jumping over the dumpster and springing over the chain link fence. I land in a squat, and his form, dressed all in black, charges down the street. He's fast, but I can do better. I take a deep breath and take off again. Air fills my burning lungs, and I pump my arms. My legs are going faster than ever before.

I never take my eyes off of him. When he rounds the corner toward a shopping center, I pray I won't lose him in the crowd. I push myself even harder and nearly trip over my own feet as I round the same corner. He's in the crowd. He's slowed down and winded but still ahead of me and about to step into the parking lot, maybe looking for his getaway vehicle.

I hurry, push on. He's only feet in front of me, but he's still moving, and I can barely breathe.

I scream with the last of my air, "Rex!"

Pausing briefly, he turns and sees me. His face flashes with confusion, and I realize this Rex doesn't know me yet. "I shot you?"

"Wrong."

I grit my teeth and go after him swinging, hand over fist into his face, then I kick him in the gut and let him crash down onto the pavement. Lying on his stomach, he struggles to get up, and I blow my knees into his back, forcing him back down. I straddle him as people begin to take notice. I sit on him as hard as I can, so he can't escape when someone asks me…

"What's going on here?"

I glance up, tear-stricken. "He tried to kill a lady … over by the tower of records. Someone needs to call the police. He still has the gun."

I nudge his pocket with my foot and can feel its form. He didn't dump the gun. He didn't have time yet to frame my dad. He would, if given the chance, which is the only reason he hasn't jumped forward in time yet.

It is the only thing that saved me and will crucify him.

People are on their phones dialing 911. A man kneels down beside me with horror on his face.

"Honey, you shouldn't have chased him. What if he hurt you?"

I smirk. "He won't, but he works for Patricia James. She's dangerous."

The man scowls. "The CEO of Rewind?"

The crowd makes sure Rex has nowhere to go as we wait for the police. They arrive, take statements, and place him under arrest. Turns out, I wasn't the only one who saw him. An old lady reported a man matching his description running from the alley. Now the police had a reason to believe her.

Thanks to me. Thanks to my gift.

But if I want to save my family, I need to get rid of this ability. I can't travel in time anymore.

When reporters and camera crews appear, I disappear. I walk into Kmart and find a secluded aisle. I touch the fluffy towels and smile up at the security monitor watching me. I think of young Mike and Molly, Dad, Mom ... Jax. I don't know what the world holds for any of us, but I'm ready to face it.

I'm ready to leave this past behind.

Chapter Twenty-Five

Knock-knock-knock.

I open my eyes and see I'm lying in bed. Gone is the room I grew used to at Jax's house. The walls are brick, and the bed is only a double, not a queen.

I'm back in Charlestown.

But this room is bigger than the one I had at home with Dad. The knock continues, and I lean up on my elbows when the door opens. Dad sticks his head in.

"They'll be here soon. You want to think about getting out of that bed?"

"Dad."

My throat croaks. I jump out of bed and leap to him, wrapping my arms around his neck. I take a deep breath and inhale his musky aftershave. His arms wrap around me in a big bear hug, the kind I remembered. It feels like years since I've felt his hug, years. And I'm sorry I wanted to trade them in, so sorry. I want to tell him all that, but I don't.

I don't.

"Well, usually morning wake-ups don't get me such a warm reception. Usually, it's mumbling and growling."

"I don't growl," I smirk. "Sparky growls." I pretend to roll my eyes, but I don't think it's convincing.

Dad looks at me as if I were growing an extra head. "Well, get dressed. Then we can have some breakfast before your ride gets here."

When he leaves, I bounce into action. I'm thrilled to see my wardrobe no longer resembles Barbie dolls. All the rhinestones are gone, but some sparkles remain. Dressing in some jeans and a sparkly top is a lot easier than skinny jeans and platform pumps.

This I can do.

I keep my hair loose and curly and pick up my purse in the corner of the room and go through my possessions. My phone is black again, and inside my wallet I find my student ID.

Lara Crane.

I squeeze my eyes shut and say a thankful prayer. I hurry to breakfast with Dad. We're alone, and I enjoy his burnt toast, eggs, and juice. My favorite pup resides under the table between my legs and I feed him bits of my bacon. He's happy, and I am too. Scratching the top of Sparky's head, I smile at Dad. I hear a squeak from the next room, and Dad stands.

"Oh, she's finally up."

He goes back into the kitchen, and I turn to see Mom standing there in her flannel pajamas. She rubs her belly. It's big. Pregnant. I gawk at her.

"Mom," I whisper and run to her.

She hugs me the best she can. "Good morning, princess. We finally decided what we would name her. It came to us last night."

"Molly," I say, incredulously.

She smiles back—soft, angelic. "Molly." She kisses my forehead, and I put a hand to her belly, where my baby sister kicks. "Sit with me while I have breakfast, okay?"

She lowers herself into the seat and rests her hands on top of her belly. "Where are you off to today?"

"School," I answer, hoping it's the right one.

Dad comes back in and puts a plate of eggs and toast in front of her.

"Thank you," she says with a big smile and rubs his cheek. "You're too good to me, John."

He kisses her as though he loves her more than life itself. "Who knew that we, at this age, would be getting ready to become parents again?"

Mom glows. "I always wanted to be a stay-at-home mom for Lara, but I couldn't do that. Now I can."

"You don't work?"

Mom looks offended. "I work. Here. It's not easy growing a new human being, you know, and keeping up with you and all your activities." She bites into her toast.

"Sorry, I didn't mean anything by it."

She smiles at me. "Go wash up for school. Your friend will be here soon."

I almost forgot to brush my teeth. I rush to the bathroom, flick on the light, and find my toothbrush. Something about my reflection bothers me. I pull back my hair and see a pinhole mark on my neck where I was shot. But that was in a different timeline. That should have faded like my bullet wound when I was shot in the alley. Shouldn't it have?

What is going on?

My teeth clean, I put my toothbrush down and put the toothpaste back into the medicine cabinet. When I shut the door, I prick my finger on the sharp corner. I grimace, and a small spot of blood appears. I feel my blood pressure rise, and the room blurs and fills with fog.

Suddenly, I'm not standing in the bathroom. I'm in a large, sterile room strapped to a gurney. Machines are beeping, and I can barely catch my breath as my heart races out of control. Tight straps hold my hands and arms still. Needles prickle my body at dozens of entry points. My eyes are dried like peeled grapes, and I can't even blink. All I can do is arch my back when I strain.

People run around in a panic. "She's waking up. She's waking up!"

My back arches. "Let me go! Help me!"

Rex leans over my face. He strokes my hair back. His voice is soft, soothing and it makes my skin crawl. "Relax, Lara. Relax. Your Uncle Rex is here. He's going to take good care of you, I promise." He snarls as he looks up at someone else in the room. "Inject her again."

"It seems she's resistant to the—"

"I don't care. Then give her twice the dose. Three times. Whatever it takes."

Something slips beneath my skin, and a moment later I am rubbing my forehead. When I open my eyes, I am sitting in the car with Rick. I glance around, unsure how I got here and where I'm going, but I'm with Rick, which is what I wanted, so why is there so much dread? Why am I so upset?

He parks the car in the high school parking lot, then he turns it off and faces me. His hand plays with my hair, which feels nice. I close my eyes as he edges in for a kiss. Our lips meet, and everything about it is perfect. I've missed him so much, but my mind flashes to Donovan. My heart wrenches with guilt, and when I think I have everything I want, I pull away.

"What's wrong, Lara? You've been acting funny since I picked you up."

I doubt I'll ever act the same again, not unless they can scrub my mind and I can forget everything I've seen and done over the past few days.

"Sorry, I have a headache. And Mom … is getting close to having her baby. A lot going on at home. I'm glad you're here though." I give him a smile.

When he returns it, I know he's bought my words. To clinch the deal, I lean forward and kiss him again, ignoring the pang of guilt in my chest. I feel as if I'm eating the last cookie in the package that someone else was saving.

I had Rick, I had Donovan, and now I have Rick again. Silly as it is, I'm sorry for the Lara that lost Donovan, almost as though she were a separate person from me. She was so distinct, but I have all her memories. She was and wasn't me at the same time. It's hard to rationalize and make sense of any of it, so I'm simply not going to think about it anymore.

"Walk me to my locker?"

Rick nods, and when we get out of the car he slings his arm over my shoulder. It seems to belong there.

Once we're inside, Kristine appears from nowhere grinning and bouncing on her feet. The girl never seems to change, no matter what timeline we're in.

"Hey guys! I thought you were going to miss English again."

"Not again."

I head over to my locker, unsure whether I'll remember my combination, but I spin the dial, and the numbers come to me. My books tumble out. I bend over to pick them up.

"Let me help you," Rick says and hands me a few books. A blue piece of paper is lying on the ground. He picks it up and unfolds it.

My heart stills. I recognize the stationery.

"What's this mean?" He hands it to me.

I recognize the handwriting. I should. It's mine.

It's not over.

I want it to be over. I don't want to live this time travel hopping life anymore. If saving Mom, Dad, and Molly wasn't enough to make me happy, what will be?

"What's it mean?" Rick asks.

I shrug. "Who knows. Some kid probably put it in my locker." I crumble it up and throw it back in and slam the door shut.

****

In class everyone acts as if I should be there, but I don't belong. I go through the motions, and take out my books, and find my pencil, but right when I think I'm settled, Donovan strolls into class.

My chest pangs. He's cool and suave. From his dark sunglasses to his arrogant swagger, everything about him is what I used to hate, but now when I see it, I want to run to him.

He takes the seat across from me, lays out his notebook, and takes his sunglasses off. He looks at me, and his eyes bore a hole into my soul.

"Do you have a spare pen?"

"Me?" My voice chokes. "No. Sorry."

He grunts and throws an arm over the back of his chair to wink at a girl in another row. This Donovan is a player, a playboy in the eleventh grade. I miss the serious, warm, and caring boy I knew.

"Well, thanks anyway. It's Crane, right?"

"Lara." I hold my hand out, feeling like a geek, but he shakes it anyway.

"Your mom's Miranda, right? Pretty sure my mom told me we played as kids a few times, before your mom quit working." He sucks on his lip and whistles. "Too bad."

"Too bad my mom quit working or too bad we stopped playing together?"

He smirks so his dimples are exposed. "Maybe both."

I laugh and shake my head. The teacher begins talking, and I turn to the front, but I barely hear him. He may as well be one of those *WAH-WAH-WAH* adults from Charlie Brown. My eyes focus on the wall clock. The hands are spinning backwards. At first I think it's only the second hand, but then I realize it's also the minute hand. Time is going backwards. I turn in my seat and look at the other students, but no one else seems to notice. I sit straight ahead and blink. It's turning clockwise again.

I'm losing my mind.

Rubbing my forehead, I wish I knew what was going on.

"Please open your books to page 245."

Sighing, I flip my book open, but all my pages are blank, like a journal. Half the class stares at me as I slam my book shut. The teacher puts his hands on his hips, and his cheeks turn the shade of his bald, sunburned head. I slouch in my seat and open my book back up, but this time the words are filled in.

I can't take it anymore. I'm up from my desk and running down the hall. I find the girl's restroom and slam the door shut. I lean against it and close my eyes. Taking a deep breath, I try to calm down. I rush to the sink and splash water on my face. I don't know what's going on with me or who I can talk to who will make it better. Maybe no one. Maybe this is my punishment for mucking with time.

I cup my hand to collect water and drink it. Feeling better and more in control, I straighten up and glance in the mirror. Someone steps behind me.

It's the woman with the purple hair.

Chapter Twenty-Six

She was spotted at my dad's prison. My mother called her a ghost. I warned Mike about her.

And now she's standing right in front of me.

I pivot on my heel to face the woman that appeared behind me. Her hair is long and the purple is in streaks. She's wearing sunglasses, and her outfit is made completely of skintight leather. I don't know who she is or what she wants, but her being here is bad.

Real bad.

"Come any closer," I say, "and I'll scream."

She smiles, not entirely unkindly. Her gloved hands go up to her hair and pull it off. It's a wig?

"I always wear this when I'm working. Makes me more of an enigma." She shakes out her own hair, also long but in spiral curls. It looks exactly like my mom's. She takes off her sunglasses, and my knees go weak. My hands brace against the basin behind me, so I don't collapse onto the floor.

"You're me?" I say meekly.

She catches me before I fall. "You have to hang strong, Lara. You've made it this far. You can get out of this."

"Tell me what's going on. Spill it."

"You never made it out of the car with Donovan. They apprehended you before you leaped back in time. They want you to think you jumped."

"I'd remember ..." I whisper.

She shakes her head. "Memory swapping, remember? They took those memories out and put in the ones they want."

"Why?"

"They want to find the location of the video, so they can destroy it, so nothing exists any more to stop the senator and Rex."

I swallow hard and close my eyes. "So my Mom, my dad … Rick …"

"None of it is real. I know it's hard to process this, but I'm going to help you. We need to fix things."

"So in your past, Rex …" It all clicks in my mind. "In *your* past, Rex was successful. You didn't save Molly. You didn't save Dad or Mom. The Senator has the power to make time travelers out of regular men? So anyone in her way can be stopped thanks to time travel.

"Nothing went the way we wanted it to," she whispers.

"You're the one who left me the notes." I know it's true even before she nods. "Rex's men at the YMCA kidnapped me. That's why you left the notes. They brought me to the facility and did whatever they are doing to me right now."

"I'm afraid so."

"The news said you were at the prison when Dad was hurt. Did you try to kill him?"

"No, I was there to make sure he survived."

I try to swallow a frog caught in my throat. "So if they have me, how do I get out? Won't I … be turned into you?"

"There's still time for you to wake up and save Molly, everyone. But it isn't going to be easy."

I nod and listen.

"Chaos is going on out there while you're in here. Rewind is being raided for illegal tests on humans. Donovan is searching for you. Our father heard word that you were kidnapped and broke out of the hospital to find you."

I squeeze my eyes shut. So much damage. So much pain. "Is there any way to go back further? To fix it?"

"This is as far back as we can go without messing it up worse. I've done all I can to get you here." She makes a move backward, and fearing she's going to go away, disappear into the wall or something, I grab her arm.

"What happened to you? To us?"

Her face crumbles, but she regains composure. "Rex broke me. For me, the memories were more important than reality. I had no reality. The happy world he created was the most important thing to me, and he used them to control me, get me to do what he wanted, what they wanted."

Deep despair covers her face. "Senators, the government, I've changed so much I don't recognize the country anymore or the world. Rex got richer, and I got … nothing.

"People work, but there is no real passion. Conviction has left the world. I didn't do that by myself, but it started with me, with us. You have to stop it. Find a way out of here before the police unknowingly give power to the one woman who will destroy this country."

"How do I get out?"

"I don't know … I never found one, but I never looked. You have to do it, Lara."

"If this is all made up, a fake memory, how did you get in? How can we be talking?"

"Because I was here once." Her face looks terrified as she thinks of something I have no knowledge of yet. "This is a virtual reality I lived in once, which means it exists in the past, which means I can walk right into it. But we really need you to say goodbye. You need to get out of here. Soon." The last words spoken, right before my eyes, she disappears.

Now it's only me, and I have nowhere to go that's safe, that's home. I have to find a way out of my utopia bliss, or it's the end of me. It's the end of everything, if I can believe she's real.

If I can believe I haven't lost my mind.

Chapter Twenty-Seven

I go to lunch because I'm starving. I'm not sure how I can be hungry in a fictional world, but I am. I don't have a lot of money, but I have enough to buy a sandwich and a bottle of milk.

Socializing isn't really high on my list of things to do, so I sit alone. I unfold the wax paper my sandwich is in, and it crinkles, it feels real. But I know it's not.

Unless of course, I'm insane, and the purple lady isn't real. But I think she is. I've been wrong about a lot of things, but the one thing I have never questioned is my sanity. Maybe I need to. Maybe I should be happy with what I have.

The sandwich tastes good, and the milk quenches my thirst. How can a memory hit the spot like that? The cafeteria is loud. The kids are laughing, enjoying themselves. How can that all be made up? Maybe this reality, if you can call it that, is designed to work on memories I already have. I've drank milk and ate tuna fish a million times. I already know how they taste; it's not a new experience.

That's what I need to do. I need to find a new experience and see what happens. Like the textbook in class, maybe it'll be blank. I have to pray that's the case because if it isn't, I am pretty sure I can chalk up my entire existence as stark raving mad.

I get back in line to read the menu. I need to find something I've never eaten. The menu reads like a fast food restaurant—burgers, fries, meatball sandwiches—all of which I've had before. There's oatmeal with honey, but I can't have honey because I'm allergic. My eyes settle on the special, a veggie burger. I'm a stark supporter of eating meat and never in my darkest nightmares would I eat a burger made of beans.

That's exactly what I need.

I rifle through my backpack and can't find a single dime to my name. Frustrated, I give a loud sigh, and that's when someone clears his throat behind me.

It's Donovan. I wear shock on my face as he hands me a crumbled up five-dollar bill.

"I wouldn't want my old playmate to go hungry." He offers me a charming smile.

I thank him and buy the veggie burger. I take my tray back to the table, unable to shake Donovan, who's talking the whole way and then sits across from me.

"You've never paid attention to me before. Why aren't you hanging out with your clique of friends?" I take the top bun off my burger and remove the patty. I sit it on my tray and stare at it as a mortal enemy. It's the moment of truth, but I'm not ready to bite into it yet.

He shrugs and leans on the table. "I've noticed you. How could I not with hair and eyes like yours."

Even now he's a charmer, but if I'm sane, he's not real. He's only smoke and mirrors. If I'm insane, well … I don't really want to think about that.

"I'm with Rick," I say to keep up the illusion.

He leans back, offended. "So people tell me."

"Oh, so you're talking to other people about me?"

"I had to see what makes you tick. Why don't you tell me…?" He glances down. "You on a low-carb diet or something?"

"Not exactly."

"You have to put ketchup on it. You can't eat it like that."

"Sure I can." I smirk at him and pick up the patty. He appears nervous. I close my eyes and take a bite. It's warm and soft but tastes like nothing.

Absolutely nothing.

I can't even taste the black beans, which Dad always hid in his chili because he couldn't stand red beans. I chew, swallow, and take a sip of my milk, completely satisfied with myself.

Donovan seems to be sitting on pins and needles. "How'd it taste?"

"Perfect."

He appears relieved. The bell rings, and he says, "How about I walk you to your next class? Maybe after school I can take you out for a real burger?"

I put my hand on his chest to stop him from following me. "I know why you're here. I know why they sent you." His eyes are confused. "They thought Rick would make me happy, make me reveal where I hid the microchip, but when I didn't, when they saw how much I longed for you, they changed their plan. But it's not going to work, Donovan. I don't want … this."

"I don't know what you're talking about. Are you on meds or something?" His eyes are dark and angry.

However they are controlling the images and what people say to me, somehow their real feelings are leaking in, which means maybe my feelings can leak out. If my mind believes this is real, maybe my body will too. I think of all those cheesy movies Rick's Mom forced me to watch:

A movie where a time traveler from the 1800s found a copper penny in his pocket, from the 1970s. It broke the illusion and forced him back to his time period. I also recall an old Star Trek episode where if one of them was killed in virtual reality, they actually died because they believed in the fantasy.

Thinking back, I remember how I pricked my finger, and for a brief moment, I'm out of the dream. That's what I need to do. I need to hurt myself so badly they have to take me off the machines, remove the needles, and ensure that I get medical treatment.

I leave Donovan and return to the bathroom. I check to make sure all the stalls are empty, then wedge the bathroom door shut. I take my fist and smash the mirror. It doesn't break on the first try, so I keep going until it cracks. My knuckles hurt and are bright red, but they aren't bleeding yet.

On the next hit, it shatters. My knuckles are gorged open, and I suck in my breath. I cradle my hand and see I have a piece of glass stuck in the open wound.

Instead of pulling the glass shard out, I wiggle it around. The pain makes me scream, which does the job.

The bathroom begins to fog up, and the next breath I take is with my real lungs.

Chapter Twenty-Eight

The real world hurts much worse than my gashed knuckle.

My back arches, and I scream, eyes searching the room. I see ceiling tiles, and then hands are on my arms, trying to still my movements. But I fight, every muscle in my arm contracting.

People all around tell me it'll be okay, that everything will be fine, but I don't believe them. They want to destroy me.

My arm comes free, and I scratch someone's face. He screams and backs away. I try to sit up but can't. I flail, but my arms are pinned down. Nothing works. There's no way out.

I hear Rex. I glance up and see his smug face, stroking back my hair.

"Dear Lara, you do know how to make things hard on yourself, don't you?"

"You said this would be easy," says Patricia's familiar voice. She steps close enough for me to see her, arms crossed and face pinched in anger. "You said you could break her."

"Nothing worth doing is easy," Rex says and places a mask over my nose and mouth.

I take a deep breath and notice that it smells stale. I do my best to wiggle free, but I don't know where I would go anyway. My mind blanks out again, but instead of darkness, there is nothing.

An absence of color. An absence of existing.

Just nothing.

Chapter Twenty-Nine

"Can you hand me that streamer?"

Blinking, my hands come into view. One is bandaged, and the other is holding a pink streamer. I hand it to my father, who is balancing up high on a ladder. The room is decorated all in pink. There are balloons, streamers, and a banner that reads *Welcome our baby girl!* I don't know what's going on. I remember being at school, at lunch, but after that, nothing.

I should be doing something else, something important, but what?

"Guests will be arriving soon. Why don't you go get the punch ready?" Dad says as he hurries down the ladder. He moves it aside. "Hurry, Lara."

My head snaps, and I rush to the kitchen. I get the punch bowl out of the fridge and look for cups and a ladle. After I set up the punch bowl on the table, the doorbell rings. Guests are arriving. I welcome them and take their gifts.

Once they all arrive, we dim the lights and quietly wait for Mom to arrive. She doesn't see us when she first comes in. I think she looks beautiful in her simple sweater with her hair freshly styled from the salon.

I turn the light on, and everyone jumps out and yells, "Surprise!" Horns are tooted and confetti is thrown. Mom giggles and holds a hand to her chest. "Who decided it's a good idea to scare the pregnant woman?"

"It was my idea," I say and beam as she pulls me tight and hugs me. It's great to be so close to her.

"You are my favorite, peanut," she says and kisses the top of my head.

Dad comes in and squeezes us both in a group hug.

"I love group hugs," I say and am so happy and content, I'm not sure if I want to be anywhere else ever.

***

After all the guests are gone, I take a phone call from Rick and then help Mom hang the baby clothes on tiny hangers. The dresses are so beautiful, and the pajamas are so soft. I can't believe soon I will have a sister.

She gives me a small smile. "You were that small once, it's hard to believe. Excited?"

"I always wanted someone to grow up with. I promise I'll always take care of her."

She sits down in the rocking chair with an uncomfortable expression on her face. "I know you will. That's what is so amazing about you. You care so much. I never worry about your heart, Lara."

I put the rest of the baby clothes away, and for a moment, an image flashes in my mind of a little girl's locket. I rub my forehead.

"Are you okay?" Mom asks.

"Yeah, just a strange headache."

Concern flashes across her face. "Why don't you go lay down, and I'll bring you some medicine." She pushes herself awkwardly out of the rocking chair, while I go to my room.

The bed is comfortable, and my pillow is soft. On the nightstand, I see a photo of my tenth birthday. It's a group picture of me, Mom, Dad, and a host of different kids that all were there for my party at the bowling alley.

I smile at it and touch the glass, remembering this same photo. But in that photo, it was me and Dad. Mom wasn't around.

Because Mom was dead.

Memories and images from the last several days crush me like an oncoming freight train, leaving me paralyzed. All I can do is be still, think, and process the fact that the last few hours with my Mom, her friends, and our family was all make believe. I must get out of here and find my real Mom and Jax. So many people are worried about me, and let's face it, I have no concept of time. I don't know if I've been Rex's prisoner for hours, days, or even longer.

How long has he been trying to extract the data from me? I have no more time to lose.

I tried cutting myself, but that didn't quite get me the results I wanted. Now I am going to have to try something more extreme. But what?

Mom comes in and hands me two pills and a glass of water. "There, stay in here until you feel better. Then we'll make popcorn and put on a movie."

Sounds like a great idea, but it's not one I can stick around for. She brushes my hair away from my forehead to kiss me. I close my eyes and feel the pain of mourning this reality, even though it's only fictional. I wish I could stay here.

I ignore the pills as I swing my legs over the side of my mattress and think. Of all the things I could do to wake myself up, what would be severe enough that they would need to move me, get me off the equipment, and give my body a moment's rest? My mind flashes back to the cafeteria menu of items I had to choose from.

Honey.

I walk past the bathroom where Mom is standing, clutching her belly. "John ... Lara ... I think it's time!"

She's only a hallucination, so I ignore her and march into the kitchen. I tear through the cabinets until I find the ones with spices and sugar. I push everything out of the way and smile as I grip the bottle of honey in my hand. I study the cute little plastic bear and flip the cap open. I remember when I was six and accidentally had honey, how painful it was. I swelled up, and my throat closed in a matter of minutes.

"I guess we had the baby shower just in time!" Dad says from the hall. "Lara, get your coat; we have to get to the hospital."

Putting the bottle to my mouth, I tilt my head back. I have no idea how much is too much, but I gulp back at least a teaspoon, probably more. It tastes sweet, delicious really, and traces of it stick to my tongue.

I can't draw breath, and my cheeks begin to puff up. I don't even try to call out to my parents, afraid they'll have an EpiPen that will end my reaction. My heart races as my throat swells up so much I can't swallow or even eke out a final scream.

The world begins to turn grey, and soon a seizure will come. I fall to my knees as I lose all sense of myself and balance.

"Lara!" Dad screams and pulls me back into his arms as my body shakes.

Chapter Thirty

When my eyes open again, I am in a white sterile room with padded walls, wearing baggy pajamas. This time my room contains only my bed, a small sofa, and a table filled with magazines. There are no chains or restraints, which surprises me. It takes a moment for my legs to respond, but I am able to stand on my feet and steady myself with the furniture until I reach the table.

I find a newspaper beneath all the fashion magazines. It is crisp and has never been unfolded. The date makes me suck in my breath. If this newspaper is real, one month has gone by since I traveled back in time and changed the past.

That means I've been Rex's prisoner for more than three weeks.

I put the paper down and jump back when the door opens. It's an orderly, who appears to have a tray of food for me. I eye it suspiciously. He's a big guy and barely glances at me as he slides it on the table. "Better eat up. They need your strength back."

"Are they going to put me under again?"

He shrugs. A noncommittal frown on his face. "Doubt it. They said that approach isn't working on you. They're going to go another way."

"Another way?"

He shrugs. "Not like they tell me anything. I'm here for the paycheck."

"Yeah, thanks for that," I say, and he leaves.

The door latches with a resounding echo. I tear into my sandwich because there's a hole gnawing in my stomach. I am suspicious they could be trying to poison me, but I know they don't want me dead.

I'm no longer in a fantasy world, which is good, but how can I break free of what seems to be a guarded facility? Physical strength won't be in my favor, but I can time travel at will. That's my biggest strength, but how do I use it to get out of here?

When the orderly came in, a key card was hanging from his belt hoop. I need to get that, lock him in my prison, and find Molly all before anyone else realizes I'm free.

The room spins, and I feel as though I'm traveling backwards through space. Suddenly, I am staring at myself. She blinks when I do. I hear the click of the door, and we both turn to look.

"Better hurry and hide," Lara says to me. "I'll distract him."

Sprinting into action, I stand against the wall, where the door will hide me. It swings open and stops short of hitting me in the face. The orderly comes inside and puts the tray of food on the table where he put it before. Lara smiles at him.

"Why are you smiling?"

"Because I am going to beat your ass."

That's my cue. I spring into action, leaping through the air, and my body slams into his. Lara pins his arms down, while I snatch the keycard from his belt.

"Hurry," she says and begins to fade from existence. I run from the room before the orderly can get up and latch the door shut. I can tell from my surroundings I'm in what used to be a hospital. Of all the hospitals around, I can only think of one that was shut down—an old rehabilitation center.

I don't know how long it will take them to realize I'm gone and have a key. The only thing I can do is keep moving and hope I can escape before they realize I'm missing. I need to find Molly and fast.

At the elevator, I find a directory, but there's nothing useful. I guess I was expecting a listing for *Dangerous Lab* or *Prisoners Kept Here*. I check all the rooms and find an unguarded office with a computer and a printer. I check it for a flash drive but find nothing. Swearing under my breath, I check through the drawers. The middle drawer has a hidden compartment that I manage to slide open. I find pens, paper clips, and a simple flash drive. I take it, stick it in the laptop, and check its contents. I can't read anything off of it, which I consider a good thing. This must be what I've been looking for.

Scanning the laptop's hard drive, I find private correspondence between the senator and Rex, recorded conversations, financials, everything that links them together, including the deed for the hospital's property in Patricia's name. I copy everything to a folder, and while counting the seconds, I move it over to the flash drive.

Once it's finished, I snatch the drive and slip it into my pocket. I rush out of the office, right into Rex's waiting arms.

"You think we didn't know you would try this?"

My sneakers skid on the floor as I try to gain ground, but his arm clamps around my neck and begins to squeeze. I can't breathe! I try to bite his neck and scratch his forehead as hard as I can but to no effect. The guy is strong, tough, and trained to withstand a lot more that I can throw at him.

I think of his office, and suddenly, I'm standing in it again, snatching the flash drive from the laptop. I open the door, and instead of being seized by Rex, I kick him in the balls, and he bends over to clutch at himself.

I scoot past him and run down the hall. "You'll never reach Molly in time!" he screams.

But I'm already in a full sprint.

The bottom floor is crawling with guards, white coats, and enough people to know what I'm trying to do is beyond impossible. I duck against a wall and slide into an old examination room. I grab an old rusted scalpel for the assortment of tools laid out. I need to find Molly, now. I wait for an orderly to walk by. Snatching him, I throw him down onto the ground, cover his mouth, and hold the scalpel to his throat, gritting my teeth.

"Tell me what I need to know, or I will shove this in your throat. If you try to scream, I won't think twice. Understand?"

With eyes wide he nods his head.

"Where are they holding the little girl? Where?" I remove my hand and watch him lick his lips. He takes a long, shallow breath.

"Second floor, room 215."

Letting him go, I run toward the elevator as an alarm is triggered, probably by the orderly. As I run down the hall, a gunshot rips through my shoulder. I grunt and realize this isn't going to work. I think of an office.

I rip the flash drive from the laptop and this time knock Rex out with a paperweight ... I sprint to the elevator and go to the second floor instead of the first.

Molly's room is unguarded. Everyone is probably out looking for me; they won't suspect I found her so easily. Inside, she is strapped to a gurney and is unconscious. I push my alarm down and rush to her. I unstrap her arms and legs, take a moment to check for her locket. It's still there with the microchip still attached. I lift her unconscious body in my arms and give her a squeeze.

"Wake up," I beg in a whisper.

She only moans, but her arms wrap around my neck.

We empty into a hallway, and I hear the skidding of feet as people charge our location. I run for the emergency exit. Nurses are charging from all sides, grabbing at my sleeves, but I am pumping as hard as I can. I'm at full tilt, and nothing can stop me as Molly sobs and buries her face into my neck.

"Lara? I want Mommy!"

"Me too," I whisper, huffing for breath as I charge up the hill.

I see a subway stop not far away, but I also see a yellow cab parked on the curb. I open the passenger door and shove Molly inside. I jump in and scream, "Drive!" I glance back as the car shifts out of park. Men in suits run for their cars, and with them is Rex.

"Where to?"

"Police station. The closest one you can find." Molly lies in my arms, and I hug her.

She whimpers. "I was so scared."

I kiss the top of her head and see her locket glistening in the sunlight. I flip the heart pendant open and see the tiny computer chip I embedded against the gold.

"Me too." I smile. "But now we're all going to be okay."

Chapter Thirty-One

The police question me for what feels like hours. Molly sits on my lap and won't move or go anywhere, her face still buried in my hair. No one will tell me anything about where anyone is or what is going on, but they take the flash drive from me, and I hear talk about getting an arrest warrant. I hope that means Mom and Jax will be found soon and rescued.

I don't know whether I'm safe, if I'll ever really be safe, but I think for now Rex and Patricia are going to have enough problems on their hands without coming for me or Molly.

The police are nice to Molly and give her soda. She sips it as I pull the hair away from her face and cover her in kisses. She smiles, but it doesn't reach her eyes.

Behind me I hear a terrified voice scream, "Lara! Molly!"

We both turn and see Mom running toward us and Jax too, lingering in the background. They seem ragged from their captivity. We are out of the chair like a lightning bolt running toward their arms.

The hug is so intense we all fall on the floor. I swing my arm over her and squeeze. I was desperate to be with Mom all this time, and now I have her. She pulls my hair back.

"Oh, Lara. You were right, about your father, Jax, everything. I'm so sorry."

I press my lips together and glance at Jax over her shoulder. "I wasn't right about Jax. I was wrong. He loves us. He does."

Her face shows she's not sure about that, and I guess I can't blame her, but I hope I haven't torn our family apart. I hope maybe my dad can become part of it somehow. As Mom rocks Molly in her arms I consider how everything I did was worth it.

The police behind me mobilize. They're going after the senator. They're going to bring her in, and I hope it's enough to stop Rex. I hope for a while maybe we'll all have some peace.

"Can I see Dad?"

Mom nods and strokes my hair. "He's going to be acquitted, like you always wanted. Everything you did for him, you proved he was innocent, and I ... should' listened too. I'm sorry, Lara."

As Molly lies against Mom's chest, I realize I can't wish her away any more than I could wish myself away. I need her in my life as if she had always been part of my family.

"It wasn't all for Dad."

Molly smiles at me as she's tucked in Mom's arms. I touch her chubby cheeks, wanting nothing more than to protect her. "Can we go for sodas? Maybe burgers?" she asks.

The imagery of something so simple, so mundane, makes me laugh.

Mom wipes her eyes. "Tell you what, how about we go get Mike, and we go get those burgers? The four of us?"

My heart soars. I stand up, and we both take one of Molly's hands. "I'm sorry, Mom, if you get in trouble. If Rewind—"

"It's just a corporation. Nothing but a stupid company. I never should've let myself be manipulated by Patricia." Her voice is strong, resolute. "I have you, Molly, our family. That's all that matters." She lifts Molly up in her arms again and gives her kisses, while my sister squeezes her back like there's no tomorrow. My heart swells with happiness.

"I'm sorry it took so long for me to see it." Mom frowns and touches my face. Her thumb strokes me. "I can fix it, if there's still time."

"There's still time."

I step forward and smile at Jax. His lips are drawn and his eyes sad. His shoulders round forward like a sad boy who misses his dog, and when I call him, he barely looks up.

My arm extends, and I offer him my hand. "Maybe we should make it five burgers."

His eyes lock with mine, and he fights back tears. He nods, takes my hand, and squeezes it. Before I know it, he pulls me into his arms and crushes me into a bear hug. I wrap my arms around his waist and bury my head against him. Jax is a victim in this same as me and Mom. He has been living with his crimes for so long, I can't judge him. He did his best to protect Mom, me.

Molly hugs my leg, and Mom hugs me and Jax. We are a unit. A family.

Epilogue

"So a time traveler, huh?" Donovan asks.

We are holding hands and walking through the park. It's summer now, and I'm wearing a cozy outfit of shorts and a blue tank top.

I shrug. "It's no big whoop."

He smiles, shy and reserved. It's been so long since we've seen each other, I'm not sure what to say next. His mother is arrested and awaiting trial. That's all my fault, even if she was guilty as sin.

Donovan tucks my hair behind my ears. "You saved your mom's life, your sister's, and stopped a dangerous group from trying to shape our country, the world. I'd say pretty big whoop."

I smile.

"All that time the video was right in Rex's grasp?"

"Yup, right on Molly's locket."

He shakes his head. "And now that you're a time travel superhero, what are you going to do with your new power?"

My eyebrow arches. "I hope nothing. I hope Mom can come up with something to fix me, but even if she doesn't, I hope never to time travel again. Believe me." I take a deep breath. "Donovan, about your Mom—"

He places a finger over my lips. "How about we don't. She kidnapped you, Molly, and was ready to kill anyone who got in her way."

"She's still your mother," I whisper. "You must have things you want to get off your chest."

He holds both my hands, and we are closer to each other than we have been in ages, our chests practically touching. "How about instead of all that, I kiss you and ask you what you're doing tomorrow night for dinner?"

I smile and bite my lip. "I think I'd like that a lot more than you realize."

He grins, and when our lips meet, it's magic. I haven't forgotten Rick and how much I loved him once, but my heart belongs to Donovan. He is everything to me. I know things will be hard for him in the future with his mom's arrest, but I look forward to facing it with him.

He walks me uptown to where I'm staying with my dad for the weekend and kisses me goodbye. I go inside the small apartment and watch Dad cook mac and cheese. He doesn't see how nostalgic it makes me, but when he shows me the small yellow lab puppy he bought, I melt. "Oh, Sparky," I whisper, and the puppy comes to me. I crush it in a hug.

"I figure with all that money the government is giving me for wrongful imprisonment, I have enough to spend on a dog. What do you say?"

My dad's face is wide and full of joy. I pet the puppy, and even though I know he isn't my old dog, I'm sure we'll be great friends.

"I say it's great. I always wanted a dog."

I follow Dad into the kitchen. It's a tight fit with a table and chairs, but the room sings with love. I hug Dad around the waist, and he kisses the top of my head.

"Make things right with your boyfriend?"

He says the word with distain in a way Jax never does, but it makes me smile. He is dad. That gives him a right.

I nod. "We're going to go out tomorrow night."

"Only if you're back by nine."

"Dad!" I roll my eyes.

"Ten," he says with a twinkle in his eye. "Set the table, okay?"

I nod and head to the cabinets. The table is by the window and has a beautiful view of the city. I watch the traffic roll by with a smile on my face.

My cell phone rings. "Hi, Jax."

"Hey ... peanut. Just wanted to wish you good night. Mom and I have counseling tonight and wanted you to know we're looking forward to picking you up in a few days."

"Me too. I'll see you soon. Tell the twins I love them."

"Will do. See you soon. Tell John, well, never mind. See you soon."

When I hang up, Dad brings the food to the table. He says grace, leaning across the table so we can hold hands. "Mac and cheese still your favorite?"

"Oh, definitely!" I pick up my fork and dig in.

For a moment it feels nothing has changed. As though I never time traveled at all.

Almost.

I take a spoonful of mac and cheese to my mouth. Blowing on the steaming pasta, I look up. The clock catches my eye.

The hands are spinning backwards.

Find out what is next for Lara in the next Rewind Adventure coming soon.

Connect

Love this book? Let others know by leaving a review on Amazon, or Barnes and Noble! Not only do these help readers, but help me craft sequels and new projects.

Want to stay up to date on latest releases, exclusive news and contests? Join my newsletter

http://jillacooper.com/content/newsletter

About the Author

Jill Cooper loves tea more than coffee and is obsessed over finding that perfect recipe. She was born in 1977 and shared a room with her sister for eighteen years. Early on, she had dreams of writing romances and mysteries. It was something she did when most kids were trying out for softball or out riding bikes.

She's always loved dark mysteries, but also enjoys a great comedy so she tries to include both these things in everything she writes, one way or another.

Jill lives in Danvers, Massachusetts with two cats, a toddler, a husband, and a 1964 yellow taxi. Her life is chaotic, but fun. She can be contacted at http://www.jillacooper.com

Printed in Great Britain
by Amazon